It was the dress, Jill realized

The dress and its magic. She ran her gloved hand along the bodice with its Venetian-lace collar and row upon row of delicate pearls. The high collar was adorned with pearls, too, and the skirt flared from her waist, the hem accentuated with a flounce of lace and wide satin ribbons.

"You look so beautiful," Shelly told Jill shortly after the ceremony. "Even more beautiful than the day you first tried on the dress."

"My hair wasn't done, and I didn't have on much makeup, and I—"

"No," Shelly interrupted, "it's more than that. You hadn't met Jordan yet. It's complete now. Oh, Jill," she whispered, "you're going to be so happy...."

Jill wanted to believe that—how she wanted to believe it. But she was afraid. So very afraid of what the future held for her and Jordan.

Dear Reader,

This has been fun! For the past few months, my office has looked as though someone threw a bridal shower here. Pictures of wedding dresses and floral arrangements have crowded my desk and crept onto the top of my computer. The floor was stacked knee-deep with wedding magazines. Sample invitations were pinned to the walls.

All of this wedding paraphernalia has not only provided me with inspiration while I worked on *The Man You'll Marry*, but it's had a very practical purpose, too. My daughter Jenny and her fiancé, Kevin LaCombe, are planning to marry in July. So, writing the first book in Harlequin Romance's Bridal Collection is both an honor and a timely event in my life.

And in case you haven't guessed, I have just **the** dress for Jenny!

Sincerely,

Debbie Macomber

THE MAN YOU'LL MARRY

Debbie Macomber

Harlequin Books

TORONTO • NEW YORK • LONDON
AMSTERDAM • PARIS • SYDNEY • HAMBURG
STOCKHOLM • ATHENS • TOKYO • MILAN
MADRID • WARSAW • BUDAPEST • AUCKLAND

For Jenny and Kevin

ISBN 0-373-03196-3

Harlequin Romance first edition May 1992

THE MAN YOU'LL MARRY

CHAPTER ONE

JILL MORRISON caught her breath as she stared excitedly out the airplane window. Seattle and everything familiar was quickly shrinking from view. She settled back comfortably and sighed with pure satisfaction.

This first-class seat was an unexpected gift from the airline. The booking agent had made a mistake and Jill turned out to be the beneficiary. Not a bad way to start a long-awaited vacation.

She glanced, not for the first time, at the man sitting next to her. He looked like the stereotypical businessman, typing industriously on a lap-top computer keyboard, his brow furrowed with concentration. She couldn't tell exactly what he was doing, but noticed several columns of figures. He paused, and something must have troubled him, because he reached for the phone located on the seat between them and punched out a long series of numbers. He turned away from her to speak briskly into the receiver. When he'd finished, he returned to his computer. He seemed impatient and restless, as though he begrudged this traveling time. Not a good sign, Jill mused, when the flight to Honolulu was scheduled to take five hours.

He wasn't the talkative sort, either. In her enthusiasm before takeoff, Jill had made a couple of attempts at light conversation, but both tries had been met with the most minimal responses possible, followed by cool silence.

Great. She was stuck sitting next to this grouch for the start of a vacation she'd been planning for nearly two years. A vacation that Jill and her best friend, Shelly Hansen, had once dreamed of taking together. Only Shelly wasn't Shelly Hansen anymore. Her former college roommate was married now. For an entire month Shelly Hansen had been Shelly Brady.

Even after all this time, Jill had problems taking it in. For as long as Jill had known Shelly, her friend had been adamant about making her career as a video producer her highest priority. Men and relationships would always remain a distant second in her busy life, she'd vowed. For years Jill had watched Shelly discourage attention from the opposite sex. From college onward, Shelly had rigidly avoided any hint of commitment.

Then it had happened. Her friend met Mark Brady and the unexpected became a reality. To Shelly's way of thinking, her mother's Great-Aunt Millicent—known to everyone in the family as Aunt Milly—was directly responsible for her present happiness. She'd met her tax-accountant husband immediately after the elderly woman had mailed Shelly a "magic" wedding dress. The same dress Milly had worn herself fifty years earlier.

Both Shelly and Jill had insisted there was no such thing as magic, especially associated with a wedding dress. Magic belonged to wands or fairy godmothers, not wedding dresses. To fairy tales, not real life.

They'd steadfastly denied the ridiculous story that went along with the gown. Both refused to believe what Aunt Milly had written in her letter; no one in her right mind, they told each other, could possibly take the sweet old woman seriously. *Marry the next man you meet?* Preposterous.

Personally, Jill had found the whole story hilarious. Shelly hadn't been laughing though. Shelly, being Shelly, had overreacted, fretting and worrying, wondering if there wasn't some small chance that Milly could be right. Shelly hadn't *wanted* her to be right, but there it was—the dress arrived one day, and the next she'd fallen into Mark Brady's arms.

Literally.

The rest, as they say, is history and Jill wasn't laughing any longer. Shelly and Mark had been married in June and from all appearances were blissfully happy.

Four weeks after the wedding, Jill was jetting off to Hawaii. Not the best month to visit the tropics, but that couldn't be helped. Her budget was limited and July offered the most value for her money.

The businessman in the seat beside her leaned back and sighed deeply, pinching the bridge of his nose. Whatever problem he'd encountered earlier had persisted, Jill guessed. She must have been right, because no more than ten seconds later, he reached for the phone again and made four calls in a row. Jill had the impression this man never stopped working; even during their meal he continued his calculations. Not a moment of their flight time was wasted. If he wasn't on the phone, he was studying papers from his briefcase or typing more columns of figures into his portable computer.

An hour passed. Jill had hoped her seatmate would be the friendly sort. A couple of times, almost against her will, she found herself watching him. Although she assumed he was somewhere in his mid-thirties, he seemed older. No, she corrected, not older, but... experienced. His face managed to be pleasing to the eye despite his rugged, uneven features. She wondered fleetingly how he would assess her appearance. Except that he hadn't looked directly at her once. It was as if he was totally unaware there was someone in the seat next to him. His eyes were gray, she'd noted earlier, the color of polished steel. There was nothing soft about him. Nothing gentle, either, Jill wagered.

This was obviously a man who had it all—hand-tailored suits, Italian leather shoes, gold pen and watch. She'd bet even his plastic was gold! No doubt he lived the way he flew—first class. He was the type who had all the answers, too. The type of man who didn't question his own attitudes and beliefs....

He reminded Jill of her father, long dead, long grieved. He, too, had been an influential businessman who'd held success in the palm of his hand. Adam Morrison had fought off middle age on a gym floor. Energy was his trademark and death was an eternity away. Only it was just around the corner, and he didn't know it.

Ironic that she should be sitting next to him thirteen years after his death. Not her father, but someone so much like him it was all Jill could do not to ask when he'd last seen his family.

He must have felt her scrutiny, because he suddenly turned and stared at her. Jill blushed guiltily, bowing her head over her book, reading it with exaggerated fervor.

"Did you like what you saw?" he asked her boldly.

"I—I don't know what you mean," she said in a small voice, moving the paperback ridiculously close to her face.

For the first time since he'd taken the seat next to her, the stranger grinned. It was an odd smile, off center and unpracticed, as if he didn't often find anything to smile about.

The remainder of the flight was uneventful. Jill held her breath during the descent, until the tires bumped down on the runway in Honolulu. She wished again that Shelly was taking this trip, too. With or without her best friend, though, Jill intended to have the time of her life. She had seven glorious days to laze in the sun. Seven days to shop to her heart's content and to go sight-seeing and to swim and relax and eat glorious meals.

For months Jill had dreamed of the wonders she would see and experience. Tranquil villages, orchid plantations—oh, how she loved orchids. At night, she'd stroll along lava-strewn beaches and by day there'd be flower-cloaked canyons to explore, tumbling waterfalls and smoldering volcanoes all waiting for her. Hawaii was going to be a grand adventure, Jill could feel it in her bones.

The man beside her was on his feet the instant their plane came to a standstill. He removed his carry-on bag from the storage compartment above the seat with an efficiency that told her he was a seasoned traveler. The smiling flight attendant handed him a garment bag as he strode off the plane.

Jill followed him, watching for directions to the baggage pickup. Her seatmate's steps were crisp and purposeful. It didn't surprise her; this was a man on the go, always in a rush to get somewhere. Meet someone. Make a deal. No time to stop and smell the roses for her friend the grouch.

Jill lost sight of him when she stopped to purchase a lei at a concession stand. She draped the lovely garland of orchids around her neck and fingered the delicate string of flowers, marveling at their beauty.

Once again the reminder that adventures awaited her on this tropical island moved full sail across her heart. She wasn't the fanciful sort, nor did she possess an extravagant imagination. Not like Shelly. Yet Jill felt something deep inside her stir to life....

Shelly had become a real believer in magic, Jill mused, smiling as she bought herself a fresh slice of pineapple. For that matter, even she—ever the practical one—found herself a tiny bit susceptible to the claims of a charmed wedding dress. Just a tiny bit, though.

Jill's pulse quickened the way it did whenever she thought about what had happened between Shelly and Mark. It was simply the most romantic thing she'd ever known.

Romance had scurried past Jill several times. Currently she was dating Ralph, a computer programmer, but it was more for companionship than romance, although he'd been hinting for several months that they should start "getting serious." Jill assumed he meant marriage. Ralph was nice, and so far Jill had been able to dissuade him from discussing anything about a long-term relationship. She didn't want to hurt his feelings, but she just wasn't interested in marrying him.

However, Jill fully intended to marry someday. There'd never been any question of that. The only question was *who*. She'd dated frequently in college, but there hadn't been anyone special. Then, when she'd been hired as a pharmacist for PayRite, a drugstore chain with several outlets in the Pacific Northwest, the opportunities to meet eligible men had dwindled dramatically.

Prospects weren't exactly crowding the horizon, but Jill had given up worrying about it. She'd done a fair job of pushing the thought of a husband and family to the far reaches of her mind—until she'd made one small mistake.

She'd tried on Aunt Milly's wedding dress.

Shelly had hung the infamous dress in the very back of her closet. Out of sight, out of mind—only it hadn't worked that way. Not a minute passed that Shelly wasn't keenly aware of the dress and its alleged powers.

On an impulse, Jill had tried it on herself. To this day she didn't know what had prompted her to slip into the beautiful hand-sewn wedding dress. It was so elegant, so beautiful, with row upon row of pearls and delicate lace layered over satin.

That it fit as though it had been specifically designed for her had come as much of a surprise to

Shelly as it had to Jill. Shelly had seemed almost giddy
with relief, insisting her aunt had made a mistake and
the dress was actually meant for Jill. But by that time,
Shelly had already met Mark....

No, Aunt Milly hadn't made a mistake—the wedding dress had been meant for Shelly all along. Her
marriage to Mark proved it. Besides, given the choice,
Jill preferred to find her husband the old-fashioned
way! And really, she'd have to attribute Shelly's
meeting and marrying Mark to the power of suggestion, the power of expectation. She shook her head
and hurried off to retrieve her luggage.

Then she headed outside, intent on grabbing a taxi.
As the driver loaded her bags, she simply stood for a
moment, savoring the warm breeze, enjoying the first
sounds and sights of Hawaii. She couldn't wait to get
to her hotel. Through a friend who was a travel agent,
Jill had been able to book a room in one of the most
exclusive places on Oahu at a ridiculously low rate.

The hotel was everything the brochure had promised and more. Jill had to pinch herself when she got
to her room. The first thing she did was walk to the
sliding-glass doors that led to the lanai, a balcony
overlooking the swimming-pool area. Beyond that, the
Pacific Ocean thundered against the sandy shore. The
sight was mesmerizing, the beauty so keen, it brought
tears of appreciation to Jill's eyes.

She quickly tipped the bellhop, who'd carted up her
luggage, and returned to the view. If she never went
beyond this room, Jill would have been satisfied. She
stood at the railing, the breeze riffling her long hair
about her face.

The hotel was U-shaped, and something—a movement, a figure—caught her eye. A man. Jill glanced across the swimming pool, across the tiki-hut roof of the bar until her gaze found what she was seeking. The grouch. In a lanai directly across from her. At least she thought so. He wore the same dark suit as the man with whom she'd spent five of the most uncommunicative hours of her life.

Shelly didn't know what prompted her, but she waved. After a moment, he waved back. He stepped farther out onto the lanai and she knew beyond a doubt. Their rooms were in different sections of the hotel, but they were on the same floor, their lanais facing each other.

He held a portable phone to his ear, but he slowly lowered it.

For several moments they simply stared at one another. After what seemed like an embarrassingly long time, Jill tried to pull herself away and found she couldn't. Unsure why, unsure what had attracted her attention to the man in the first place, unsure of everything, Jill looked away.

A knock at the door distracted her.

"Yes?" she asked, opening her door. A bellhop in a crisp white uniform stood before her with a large wrapped box.

"This arrived by special courier for you earlier today, Ms. Morrison," he explained politely.

When he'd left, Jill studied the package, reading the Seattle postmark and the unfamiliar block printing. She carried it to the bed, still puzzled. She had no idea who would be mailing her anything from home. Especially since she'd only left that morning.

Sitting on the edge of the bed, she carefully unwrapped the package and lifted the lid. Her hands froze. Her heart froze. Her breath jammed in her throat. When she was able to move again, she inhaled sharply and closed her eyes.

It was Aunt Milly's wedding dress.

A letter rested on top of the tissue-wrapped dress. With trembling hands, Jill reached for it.

Dearest Jill,
Trust me, I know exactly what you're feeling. I remember so well my own emotions when I opened this very box and found Aunt Milly's wedding dress staring up at me. As you know, my first instinct was to run and hide. Instead I was fortunate enough to find Mark and fall in love.

I suppose you're wondering why I'm mailing this dress to you in Hawaii. Why didn't I simply give it to you before you left Seattle? Good question, and if I had a reasonable answer I'd be more than happy to explain.

One thing I've learned these past few months is that there's precious little logic when it comes to understanding any of this—love, fate, the magic within Aunt Milly's wedding dress. Take my advice and don't even try to make sense of it.

I suppose I should tell you what prompted me to give you the dress in the first place. I was sitting at the table the other morning, with my first cup of coffee. I wasn't fully awake yet. My eyes were closed. Suddenly you were in my mind, standing waist-deep in the blue-green water. There was a waterfall behind you and lush beautiful plants all around. It had to be Hawaii. You looked happier than I can ever remember seeing you.

There was a man with you, and I wish I could describe him. Unfortunately, he was in shadow. Read into that whatever you will. There was a certain look about you, a look I've only seen once before—the day you tried on the wedding gown. You were radiant.

This all happened a week ago. I talked to Mark about it that evening. He seemed to feel the same way I did—that the dress was meant for you. I phoned Aunt Milly and told her. She said by all means to make you the dress's next recipient.

I should probably have given you the dress then, but something held me back. Nothing I can put into words, but a feeling it would be too soon, I suppose. So I'm mailing it to you now.

My wish for you, Jill, is that you find someone to love. Someone as wonderful as Mark. Of the two of us, you've always been the sensible one. You believed in logic and common sense. But you also believed in love, long before I did. I was the skeptic there. Something tells me the man you'll marry is just as cynical as I once was. You're going to have to teach him about love, the same way Mark's taught me.

Call me as soon as you get back. I'll be waiting to hear what happens. In my heart I already know it's going to be wonderful.

Love,
Shelly

Jill read the letter twice. Her pulse quickened as her eyes lifted and involuntarily returned to the lanai directly across from her own.

The frantic pace of her heart slowed to normal.

The grouch was gone.

Jill recalled Aunt Milly's letter to Shelly. "When you receive this dress," she wrote, "the first man you meet is the man you'll marry."

So it wasn't the grouch, it was someone else. Not that she really believed in any of this. Still, her knees went unaccountably weak with relief.

After unpacking her clothes, Shelly showered and lay down for a few moments, closing her eyes. She hadn't intended to fall asleep, but when she awoke, a rosy dusk had settled. Flickering fires from the bamboo poles that surrounded the pool sent shadows dancing on her walls.

She'd seen him, Jill realized. While she slept. Her hero, her predestined husband. But try as she might, she wasn't able to bring him into clear focus. Naturally it was her imagination. Fanciful thinking. Dreams gone wild. Jill reminded herself stoutly that she didn't believe in the power of the wedding dress any more than she believed in the Easter Bunny. But it was rather nice to fantasize now and again, to pretend.

Unquestionably, there was a certain amount of anticipation created by the delivery of the wedding dress and Shelly's letter. But unlike her friend, Jill didn't expect anything to come of this. Both Jill's feet were firmly planted on the ground. She wasn't as whimsical as Shelly, nor was she as easily influenced by outside forces.

True, at twenty-eight, Jill was more than ready to marry and settle down. She knew she wanted children eventually, too. But when it came to marrying the man of her dreams, she'd prefer to find him the old trial-and-error way. She didn't need a magic wedding dress gently guiding her toward him!

Initially, Shelly had had many of the same thoughts herself, Jill remembered, but she'd married the first man she'd met after the dress arrived.

The first man you meet. She was thinking about that while she changed into a light cotton dress and sandals. She was still thinking about it as she rode the elevator down to the lobby to have a look around.

There must have been something in the air. Maybe it was because she was on vacation and feeling free of her usual routines and restraints; Jill didn't know. But for some unknown reason she found herself glancing around, wondering what man it could possibly be.

The hotel was full of possibilities. A distinguished gentleman sauntered past. An ambassador perhaps? Hmm, that might be nice, she mused. Or a politician.

Naw, she countered silently, laughing at herself. She wasn't interested in politics. Furthermore she didn't see herself as an ambassador's wife. She'd probably say the wrong thing to the wrong person and inadvertently cause an international incident.

A guy who looked like a rock star strolled her way next. Now, there was an interesting prospect, although Jill had a minor problem picturing herself married to a man who wore his hair longer than she did. He was cute, though. A definite possibility—*if* she were to take Shelly's letter seriously.

A doctor would be ideal, Jill decided. With her medical background, they were sure to have a lot in common. She scanned the lobby area, searching for someone who looked as if he'd feel at home with a stethoscope around his neck.

No luck. Nor, for that matter, did she seem to be generating much interest herself. She might as well be invisible. So much for that! These speculations were all in jest anyway. . . .

Swallowing an urge to laugh, she headed out the back of the hotel toward the pristine beach. A lazy evening stroll among swaying palms sounded just the thing.

She walked toward the ocean, removed her shoes and held them by the straps as she wandered ankle-deep into the delightfully warm water. She wasn't paying much attention to where she was going, thinking, instead, about her hopes for a family of her own. Thinking about the few truly happy memories she had of her father. The Christmas when she was five and a camping trip two years later. A picnic, once. But by the time she was eight, his success had overtaken him. It wasn't that he didn't love her or her mother, she supposed, but—

"I wouldn't go out much farther if I were you," a deep male voice called from behind her.

Jill's pulse soared at the unexpectedness of the intrusion. The silhouette of a man leaning against a palm tree captured her attention. In the darkness she couldn't make out his features, yet he seemed vaguely familiar.

"I won't," she said, trying to see who'd spoken. Whoever it was stayed stubbornly under the shadows of the tree.

From the distance Jill noted that he had the physique of an athlete. She happened to appreciate wide, powerful shoulders on a man. She stepped closer, attempting to get a better look at him without being obvious. Although his features remained hidden, his chin was tilted at an arrogant angle.

A dash of arrogance in a man was a nice touch, too.

"I wondered if you were planning to go swimming at night. Only a fool would do that."

Jill bristled. She had no intention of swimming. For one thing, she wasn't dressed for it. Before she could defend herself, however, he continued, "You look just like one of those helpless romantics who can't resist testing the water. Let me guess—this is your first visit to the islands?"

Jill nodded. She'd ventured far enough onto the beach to actually see him now. Her heart sank—no wonder he'd seemed vaguely familiar. No wonder he was vaguely insulting. For the second time in a twenty-four-hour period she'd happened upon the grouch.

"I don't suppose you took time to eat dinner, either."

"I . . . had something earlier. On the plane."

He snickered softly. "Plastic food."

"I don't know what concern it is of yours."

"None," he admitted, shrugging.

"Then my going without dinner shouldn't bother you." She bristled again at the intense way he was studying her. His mouth had twisted into a faint smile, and he seemed amused by her.

"Thank you for all your advice," she said stiffly, turning away from him and heading back toward the water.

"You're not wearing the lei."

Jill's fingers automatically went to her neck as she stopped midstep. She'd left it in her room when she changed clothes.

"Allow me." He stepped forward, removing the one from his own neck, and draped it around hers. Since this was her first visit to the islands, Jill didn't know if giving someone a lei had any symbolism attached to it. She didn't really want that kind of connection with him. Just in case.

"Thank you." She hoped she sounded adequately grateful.

"I might have saved your life, you know."

That was a ridiculous comment. "How?"

"You could have drowned."

Jill couldn't help it. She laughed. "Not very likely. I had no intention of swimming."

"You can't trust the tides here. Even this close to shore, the waves are capable of jerking your feet out from under you. You might easily have been swept out to sea."

"That's absurd."

"Perhaps," he agreed, amicably enough. "I was hoping you'd realize you're in my debt."

Ah, now they were getting somewhere. This man wasn't given to generosity. She'd bet a month's wages that he'd initiated the conversation for his own purposes. He'd had plenty of time on their flight from Seattle to advise her about swimming.

No, he was after something.

Jill should have been suspicious from the first. "What is it you want?"

He grinned that cocky, unused smile of his and nodded. Apparently this was high praise of her finely honed intuitive skills.

"Nothing much. I was hoping you'd agree to attend a small business dinner with me."

"Tonight?"

He nodded again. "You did mention you hadn't eaten."

"Yes, but..."

"It'll only take an hour or so of your time." He sounded a bit impatient, as if he'd expected her to agree to his scheme without question.

"I don't even know who you are. Why would I want to attend a dinner party with you? I'm Jill Morrison, by the way."

"Jordan Wilcox," he said abruptly. "All right, if you must know, I need a woman to come with me so I won't be forced to offend someone I can't afford to alienate."

"Then don't."

"He's not the one I'm worried about. It's his daughter. She's apparently set her sights on me and she doesn't seem capable of taking a hint."

"Well, then, it sounds as though you've got yourself a problem." Privately Jill wondered at the woman's taste.

He frowned, shoving his hands into the pockets of his formal dinner jacket. He'd changed clothes, too, but he hadn't substituted something more casual for his business suit. Quite the reverse. But then, that shouldn't have surprised her. It was always business, never pleasure, with people like him.

"I don't know what it is about you women," he said plaintively. "Can't you tell when a man's not interested?"

"Not always." Jill was beginning to feel a bit cocky. She swung her shoes at her side. "In other words you need me as a bodyguard."

Clearly he didn't approve of her terminology, but he let it pass. "Something like that."

"Do I have to pretend to be madly in love with you?"

"Good heavens, no."

Jill hesitated. "I'm not sure I brought along anything appropriate to wear."

He reached inside his pocket and pulled out a thick wad of cash. He peeled away several one-hundred dollar bills and stuffed them into her hand. "Buy yourself something. The shop in the hotel's still open."

CHAPTER TWO

"I'LL PAY for the dress myself," Jill insisted for the tenth time. She couldn't believe she'd agreed to attend this dinner party with Jordan. Not only didn't she know the man, she didn't even like him.

"I'll pay for the dress," he replied, also for the tenth time. "It's the least I can do."

They were in the ultraexpensive dress shop located off the hotel lobby. Jill was shifting judiciously through the rack of evening gowns. Most were outrageously priced. She found a simple one she thought might flatter her petite build, ran her hand down the sleeve until she reached the white tag, then sighed. The price was higher than any of the others. Grumbling under her breath, she dropped the sleeve and continued her search.

Jordan glanced impatiently at his watch. "What's wrong with this one?" He held up an elegant cocktail dress. The bodice was covered with bright green sequins, and the dark green skirt was straight and slim. Lovely indeed, but hardly worth a week's salary.

"Nothing's wrong with it," she answered absently as she flipped through the row of dresses.

"Then buy it."

Jill glared at him. "I can't afford five-hundred dollars for a dress I'll probably only wear once."

"I can," he returned between clenched teeth.

"I *won't* allow you to pay for my dress."

"The party's in thirty minutes," he reminded her sharply.

"All right, all right."

He sighed with obvious relief and reached for the dress. Jill's hand on his forearm stopped him.

"Obviously nothing here is going to work. I'll check what I brought along with me. Maybe what I have is more suitable than I thought."

Groaning, he followed her to the elevator. "Wait in the hall," she instructed as she unlocked her door. She wasn't about to let a strange man into her hotel room. She stood by the closet and rooted through the dresses she'd unpacked that afternoon. The only suitable one was an antique white shirtwaist with large gold buttons and a wide gold belt. It wasn't exactly what one would wear to an elegant dinner party, but it was passable.

She raced to the door and held it up for Jordan. "Will this do?"

The poor man looked exasperated. "Hell, I don't know."

Leaving the door open, Jill raced back to scan her closet. "The only other dress I have is Aunt Milly's wedding gown," she muttered.

"You packed a wedding dress?" His gray eyes lit up with amusement. It seemed an effort not to laugh outright. "You apparently have high hopes for this vacation."

"I didn't bring it with me," she informed him primly, sorry she'd even mentioned it. "A friend had it delivered."

"You're getting married?"

"Not exactly. I— Oh, I don't have time to explain."

Jordan eyed her as if he had plenty of questions, but wasn't completely sure he wanted to ask them.

"Wear the one you showed me, then," he said testily. "I'm sure it'll be fine."

"All right, I will." By now Jill regretted agreeing to attend this dinner party. "I'll only be a minute." She closed the door again, but not before she got a glimpse of the surprised look on Jordan's face. It wasn't until she'd slipped out of her sundress that she realized he probably wasn't accustomed to women who left him waiting in the hallway while they changed clothes.

Although she knew Jordan was impatient, Jill took a few extra minutes to freshen her makeup and run a brush through her shoulder-length brown hair. Using a gold clip, she pinned it up in a simple chignon. Despite herself, she couldn't help feeling excited about this small adventure. There was no telling whom she might meet tonight.

Drawing in a deep breath to calm herself, she smoothed the skirt of her dress, then walked slowly to the door. Jordan was waiting for her, his back against the opposite wall. He straightened when she appeared.

"Will this do?"

His gaze narrowed assessingly. His scrutiny made Jill feel uncomfortable, and she held herself stiff and straight. At last he nodded.

"You look fine," was all he said.

Jill heaved a sigh of relief, returned to her room long enough to retrieve her purse, and then joined Jordan. She tested the door to be sure it was locked.

The dinner party, as Jordan had explained earlier, was in a private room in one of the hotel's restaurants. Jordan led the way to the elevator, his pace urgent.

"You'd better explain what you want me to do," she said.

"Do?" he repeated with a frown. "Hell, just do whatever it is you women do to let one another know a certain man is off-limits, and make sure Suzi understands." He hesitated. "Only do it without fawning all over me."

"I wouldn't dream of it," Jill said, gazing up at him in mock adoration and fluttering her long lashes.

Jordan's frown deepened. "None of that, either."

"Of what?"

"That thing with the eyes." He motioned with his hand, looking annoyed.

"Should I know something about who's attending the party?"

"Not really," he answered impatiently.

"What about you?" He shot her a puzzled look, and Jill elaborated. "If I'm your date, it makes sense

I'd know who you are—something beyond your name, I mean—and what you do."

"I suppose it does." He buried his hands in his pockets. "I'm the CEO for a large development company based in Seattle. Simply put, we develop projects, gather together the financing, arrange for the construction, and then once the project is completed, we sell."

"That sounds interesting." If you thrived on tension and pressure, that is.

"It can be," was his only response. He looked her over once more, but his glance revealed neither approval nor reproach.

"I didn't like you when we first met." Jill didn't know why she felt obliged to explain this. In fact, she still didn't like him, though she had to admit he was a very attractive man indeed. "I sat next to you during the flight, and I thought you were most unfriendly," she continued.

"I take it your opinion of me hasn't changed?" He cocked one brow with the question, as if to suggest her answer wouldn't trouble him one way or the other.

Jill ignored him. "You don't like women very much, do you?"

"They have their uses."

He said it in such a belittling, negative way that Jill felt a flash of hot color invade her cheeks. She turned to look at him, feeling almost sorry for a man who had everything yet seemed so empty inside. "What's made you so cynical?"

He glanced at her again, a bit scornfully. "Life."

Jill didn't know what to make of that response, but luckily the elevator arrived just then.

"Is there anything else I should know before we arrive?" she asked once they were inside. Her role, Jill understood, was to protect him from an associate's daughter. She wasn't sure how she was supposed to manage that, but she'd think of something when the time came.

"Nothing important," he answered. He paused, frowning. "I'm afraid the two of us might arouse a bit of curiosity, though."

"Why's that?"

"I don't generally associate with... innocents."

"Innocents?" He made her sound like one of the pre-school crowd. No one she'd ever known could insult her with less effort. "I'm over twenty-one, you know!"

He laughed outright at that, and Jill stiffened, regretting—probably not for the last time—that she'd ever agreed to this.

"I think you're wonderful, too," she said sarcastically.

"So you told me before."

The elevator arrived at the top floor of the hotel, where the restaurant was located. Jordan spoke briefly to the maître d', who led them to the dinner party.

Jill glanced around the simple, elegant room, and her heart did a tiny somersault. All the guests were executive types, the men in dark suits, the women in sophisticated dresses that could all have been bought from that little boutique downstairs. Everyone had an aura of prosperity and power.

Jill's breath came in shallow gasps. She was miles out of her league. These people had money, real money, whereas she'd spent months just saving for this vacation. Her money was invested in panty hose and frozen dinners, not property and office towers and massive stock portfolios.

Jordan must have felt her unease, because he turned to her and smiled briefly. "You'll be fine."

It amazed Jill how three little words from him could give her an immeasurable boost of confidence. She smiled her appreciation and drew herself up as tall and proud as her five-foot-three-inch frame would allow.

Waiters carried trays of delicate hors d'oeuvres and narrow etched-glass champagne flutes filled with sparkling, golden liquid. Jill reached for a glass and took her first sip, widening her eyes in surprise. Never had she tasted anything better.

"This is excellent."

"It should be, at a hundred and fifty dollars a bottle."

Before Jill could comment, an older, distinguished-looking gentleman detached himself from a younger colleague and made his way from across the room toward them. He was probably close to fifty, but could have stepped off the pages of *Gentlemen's Quarterly.*

"Jordan," he said in a hearty voice, extending his hand, "I'm delighted you could make it."

"I am, too."

"I trust your flight was uneventful."

Jordan's gaze briefly met Jill's. "Very pleasant. I'd like you to meet Jill Morrison. Jill, Dean Lundquist."

"Hello," she said pleasantly, extending her hand.

"Delighted," Dean said again, turning to smile at her. He took her hand and held it considerably longer than good manners required. Jill had the impression she was being carefully inspected and did her utmost to appear composed.

Finally, he released her hand and nodded toward the entrance. "If you'll both excuse me a moment, Nicholson's just arrived."

"Of course," Jordan agreed politely.

Jill waited until Dean Lundquist was out of earshot. Then she leaned toward Jordan and whispered, "Suzi's dad?"

Jordan made a wry face. "Smart girl."

Not really, since few other men would have had cause to inspect her so closely, but Jill didn't discount the compliment. She wasn't likely to receive that many, at least not from Jordan.

"Who was that standing with him?" She inclined her head in the direction of a tall, good-looking young man. Something about him didn't seem quite right. Nothing she could put her finger on, but it was a feeling she couldn't shake.

"That's Dean, Junior," Jordan explained.

Jill noticed the way Jordan's mouth thinned and the thoughtful, preoccupied look that came briefly into his eyes. "He's being groomed by Daddy to take my place."

"Junior?" Jill studied the younger man a second time. "I don't think you'll have much of a problem."

"Why's that?"

She shrugged, not sure why she felt so confident of that. "I can't picture you losing at anything."

His gaze swept her warmly. "I have no intention of giving Junior the opportunity, but the time's fast approaching when I'm going to have one hell of a fight on my hands."

"Just a minute," Jill said, tapping her finger against her lower lip. "If Suzi is Dean, Senior's daughter, then wouldn't a marriage between you two secure your position?" It wouldn't exactly be a love match, but she couldn't envision Jordan marrying for something as commonplace as love.

Jordan gave her a quick, unreadable look. "It'd help, but unfortunately I'm not the marrying kind."

Jill had guessed as much. She doubted there was time in his busy schedule for love or commitment, just for work, work, work. Complete one project and start another. She knew the pattern.

Jill couldn't imagine herself falling in love with someone like Jordan. And she couldn't picture Jordan in love at all. As he'd said, he wasn't the marrying kind.

"Jordan." A woman's shrill voice sent a chill up Jill's spine as a beautiful blonde raced past her and straight into Jordan's unsuspecting arms, locking him in a tight embrace.

"This must be Suzi," Jill said conversationally from behind the woman who was squeezing Jordan for all she was worth.

Jordan's irate eyes found hers. "Do something!" he mouthed.

Jill was enjoying the scene far too much to interrupt Suzi's passionate greeting. While Jordan was occupied, Jill reached for a hors d'oeuvre from a nearby silver platter. Whatever it was tasted divine, and she automatically reached for two more. She hadn't realized how hungry she was. Not until she was on her third cracker did she realize she was sampling caviar.

"Oh, darling, I didn't think you'd ever get here," Suzi said breathlessly. Her pretty blue eyes filled with something close to hero worship as she gazed longingly up at Jordan. "Whatever took you so long? Didn't you know I'd been waiting hours and hours and hours for you?"

"Suzi," Jordan said stiffly, disentangling himself from the blonde's embrace. He straightened the cuffs of his shirt. "I'd like you to meet Jill Morrison, my date. Jill, this is Suzi Lundquist."

"Hello," Jill said before reaching for yet another cracker. Jordan's look told her this was not the time to discover a taste for Russian caviar.

Suzi's big blue eyes widened incredulously. She really was lovely, but one glimpse and Jill understood Jordan's reluctance. Suzi was very young, twenty at most, and terribly vulnerable. She had to admire his tactic of putting the girl off without being unnecessarily rude.

Jordan had made Dean Lundquist's daughter sound like a vamp. Jill disagreed. Suzi might be a vamp-in-training, but right now she was only young and headstrong.

"You're Jordan's date?" Suzi asked, fluttering her incredible lashes—which were almost long enough to create a draft in the room, Jill decided.

She smiled and nodded. "We're very good friends, aren't we, Jordan?" She slipped her arm in his and gazed up at him, ever so sweetly.

"But I thought—I hoped..." Suzi turned to Jordan who'd edged himself closer to Jill, draping his arm across her shoulders as though they'd been an item for quite some time.

"Yes?"

Suzi glanced from Jordan to Jill and then back to Jordan. Tears brimmed in her bright blue eyes. "I thought there was something special between us...."

"I'm sorry, Suzi," he said gently.

"But Daddy seemed to think..." She left the rest unsaid as she slowly backed away. After three short steps, she turned and dashed out of the room. Jill popped another cracker into her mouth.

Several people were looking in their direction, though Jordan seemed unaware of it. Jill, however, keenly felt the interested glances. Not exactly a comfortable feeling, especially when one's mouth was full of caviar.

After an awkward moment, conversation resumed, and Jill was able to swallow. "That was dreadful," she muttered. "I feel sorry for the poor girl."

"Frankly, so do I. But she'll get over it." He turned toward Jill. "A lot of help you were," he grumbled. "You were stuffing down crackers like there was no tomorrow."

"This is the first time I've tasted caviar. I didn't know it was so good."

"I didn't bring you along to appraise the hors d'oeuvres."

"I served my purpose," Jill countered. "But I'm not happy about it. She's not a bad kid."

"Believe me," Jordan insisted, his face tightening, "she *will* get over it. She'll pout for a while, but in the end she'll realize we did her a favor."

"I still don't like it."

Now that her mission was accomplished, Jill felt free to examine the room. She wandered around a bit, sipping her champagne. The young man playing the piano caught her attention. He was good. Darn good. After five years of lessons herself, Jill knew talent when she heard it. She walked over to the baby grand to compliment the pianist, and they chatted briefly about music until she noticed Jordan looking for her. Jill excused herself; their meal was about to be served.

Dinner was delicious. Jill was seated beside Jordan, who was busy carrying on a conversation with a stately looking gentleman on his other side. The man on her right, a distinguished gentleman in his mid-sixties, introduced himself as Andrew Howard. Although he didn't acknowledge it in so many words, Jill realized he was the president of Howard Pharmaceuticals, now retired. Jill pointed out that PayRite

Pharmacy, where she worked, carried a number of his company's medications, and the two of them were quickly involved in a lengthy conversation. By the time dessert was served Jill felt as comfortable with Mr. Howard, as if she'd known him all her life.

Following a glass of brandy, Jordan seemed ready to leave.

"Thank you so much," she told Mr. Howard as she slid back her chair. "I enjoyed our conversation immensely."

He stood with her and clasped her hand warmly. "I did, too. If you don't mind, I'd like to keep in touch."

Jill smiled. "I'd enjoy that. And thank you for the invitation."

Then she and Jordan exchanged good-nights with her dinner companion and headed for the elevator. Jordan didn't speak until they were inside.

"What was that all about with Howard?"

"Nothing. He invited me out to see his home. Apparently it's something of a showplace."

"He's a bit old for you, don't you think?"

Jill gave him an incredulous look. "Don't be ridiculous. He assumed you and I knew each other. He just wanted me to feel welcome, I suppose." She didn't mention that Jordan had spent the entire dinner talking with a business associate. He seemed to have all but forgotten she was with him.

"Howard invited you to his home?"

"Us, actually. You can make your excuses if you want, but I'd really like to take him up on his offer."

"Andrew Howard and my father were good friends. My father passed away several years back, and Howard likes to keep track of the projects I'm involved with. He's gone in on the occasional deal."

"He's a sweet man. Did you know he lost his only son to cancer? It's the reason his company has done so much in the field of cancer research. His son's death changed the course of his life."

"I had no idea." Jordan was obviously astounded that he'd known Andrew Howard for so many years and not realized he'd lost a child. "You learned this over dinner?"

"Good grief, dinner lasted nearly two hours." She sighed deeply and pressed her hands to her stomach. "I'm stuffed. I'll never sleep unless I walk off some of this food."

"It would've helped if you hadn't eaten half the hors d'oeuvres by yourself."

Jill decided to ignore that comment.

"Do you mind if I join you?" Jordan surprised her by asking.

"Not in the least, as long as you promise not to make any more remarks about hors d'oeuvres. *Or* lecture me about the dangers of swimming at night."

Jordan grinned. "You've got yourself a deal."

They walked through the lobby and out of the hotel toward the beach. The surf thundered against the shore, slapping the sand, then retreating. Jill found the rhythmic sounds relaxing.

"What sort of project do you have planned for Hawaii?" she ventured after a few minutes.

"A shopping complex."

Although he'd answered her question, his expression was preoccupied. "Why the frown?" she asked.

He shot a quick glance her way. "The Lundquists seem to have some sort of hidden agenda," he said.

"You said Daddy's grooming Junior to take your place," Jill prompted.

"It looks like I'm headed for a proxy fight, which is an expensive and costly proposition for everyone involved. For now, I have the controlling interest, but by no means do I have control."

"This trip to Hawaii . . . ?"

"It's strictly business. I just wish I knew what the hell was going on behind my back."

"I wish you the best." This was a world far removed from Jill's.

"Thanks." He grinned, and suddenly seemed to leave his worries behind.

They strolled for several minutes in companionable silence. The breeze was warm, the moon full and bright, and the rhythm of the ocean waves went on and on.

"I suppose I should go back," Jill said reluctantly. She had a full day planned, beginning first thing in the morning, and although she didn't feel the least bit tired, she should think about getting some sleep.

"Me, too."

They altered their meandering course in the direction of the hotel, their shoes sinking into the moist sand.

"Thanks for your help with Suzi Lundquist."

"Anytime. Just say the word and I'll be there, especially if there's caviar involved." She felt guilty, however, about the young and vulnerable Suzi. Jordan had been gentle with her; nevertheless, Jill's sympathy went out to the girl. "I can't help feeling bad for Suzi."

Jordan sighed. "The girl just won't take no for an answer."

"Do you?"

"What do you mean?"

Jill stopped a moment to collect her thoughts. "I don't understand finance, but it seems to me that you'd never get anywhere if you quit at the first stumbling block. Suzi takes after her father and brother. She saw what she wanted and went after it. Rather an admirable trait, I guess. I suspect you haven't seen the last of her."

"Probably not, but I won't be here more than a few days. I should be able to avoid her in that time."

"Good luck." She hesitated when they reached the pathway, bordered by vivid flowering shrubs, that led to the huge lighted swimming pool.

Jordan grinned. "What with one thing and another, I have the feeling I'm going to need it."

The night couldn't have been more perfect. It seemed such a shame to waste these warm romantic moments, but Jill finally forced herself to murmur a good-night.

"Here," Jordan said just as she did.

Jill was startled when he presented her with a single lavender orchid. "What's this for?"

"In appreciation for all your help."

"Actually, I should be the one thanking you. I had a wonderful evening." It beat the heck out of sitting in front of her television and ordering dinner from room service, which was exactly what she'd planned. She held the flower under her nose and breathed in the delicate scent.

"Enjoy your stay in Hawaii."

"Thank you, I will." Her itinerary was full for nearly every day. "I might even see you...around the hotel."

"Don't count on it. I'm headed back to Seattle in two days."

"Goodbye, then."

"Goodbye."

Neither moved. Jill didn't understand why. They'd said their good-nights—there seemed nothing left to say. It was time to leave. Time for her to return to her room and sleep off the effects of an exceptionally long day.

She made a decisive movement, but before she could turn away, his hand at her shoulder stopped her. Jill's troubled gaze met his. "Jordan?"

He captured her chin, his touch light but firm.

"Yes?" she whispered, her heart in her throat.

"Nothing." He dropped his hand.

Jill was about to turn away again when he stepped toward her, took her by the shoulders and kissed her. Jill had certainly been kissed before, and the experience had always been pleasant, if a bit predictable.

Not this time.

Exciting, unfamiliar sensations raced through her. Jordan's mouth feasted on her with practiced ease while his hands roved her back, caressing slowly, confidently.

Jill was breathless and weak when he finally broke away. He stared down at her with a perplexed look, as if he'd shocked himself by kissing her. As if he didn't know what had come over him.

Jill didn't know, either. There was a sinking feeling in the pit of her stomach, and then she remembered something Shelly had told her—the overwhelming sensation she'd experienced the first time Mark had kissed her. From that moment on, Shelly had known her fate was sealed.

Jill had never felt anything that even came close to what she'd just felt in Jordan's arms. Was it possible? *Could* there be something magical about Aunt Milly's wedding dress? Jill didn't know. She didn't want to find out, either.

"Jill?"

"Oh, no," she moaned as she looked up at him.

"Oh, no," Jordan echoed, apparently amused. "I'll admit women have reacted when I've kissed them, but no one's ever said that."

She barely heard him.

"What's wrong?"

"The dress . . ." Jill stopped herself in time.

"What about the dress?"

Jill knew she wasn't making any sense. The whole thing was preposterous. Ridiculous. Unbelievable.

"What about the dress?" he repeated.

"You wouldn't understand." She had no intention of explaining it to him. She could just imagine what someone like Jordan Wilcox would say when he heard about Aunt Milly's wedding dress.

CHAPTER THREE

JILL GLARED at Jordan. He had no idea how devastating she'd found his kiss. And the worst of it was, *she* had no idea why she was feeling this way.

"Jill?" he said, eyeing her suspiciously. "What's my kissing you got to do with a dress?"

She squeezed her eyes shut, then opened them. "It hasn't got anything to do with it," she blurted without thinking, then quickly corrected herself. "It's got everything to do with it." She knew she was overreacting, but she couldn't seem to help herself. Good grief, all he'd done was kiss her! There was no reason to behave like a fool. She had a good excuse, however. It had been a long and unusual day compounded by Shelly's letter and the arrival of the wedding dress. Who wouldn't be flustered? Who wouldn't be confused—especially in light of Shelly's experience?

"You're not speaking too clearly," Jordan reminded her.

"I know. I'm sorry."

"Could you explain yourself?" he added patiently.

Jill didn't see how that was possible. Jordan, so much a man of the world, wouldn't understand a matter of the heart. Not only that, he was cynical and scornful. The man who owned the keys to yuppiedom, who placed power and profit above all else, would laugh at something as absurd as the story about this wedding dress.

She drew in an unsteady breath. "There's nothing I can say."

"Was my kiss so repugnant to you?" It didn't appear that he was going to graciously drop the matter, not when his male ego was on the line.

Forcing her voice to sound light and carefree, Jill placed a hand on his shoulder and looked him square in the eye. "I'd think a man of your vast experience would be accustomed to having women crumple at his feet."

"Don't be ridiculous." His habitual frown snapped into place.

"I'm not," she countered smoothly. Best to keep Jordan in the dark, otherwise he might misread her intentions. Besides, he wouldn't be any more enthusiastic about a romance between them than she was. "The kiss was very nice," she admitted grudgingly.

"And that's bad?" He rubbed a frustrated hand along his blunt, determined-looking jaw. "Perhaps you'll feel better once you're in your room."

Jill nodded eagerly. "Thank you. For dinner," she added, remembering her manners.

"Thank you for joining me. It was... a pleasure meeting you."

"You, too."

"I probably won't see you again."

"That's right," she agreed resolutely. No reason to tempt fate. She was beginning to like him and that could be dangerous. "You'll be gone in a couple of days, won't you? I'm here for the week." She retreated a couple of steps. "Have a safe trip home, and don't work too hard."

They parted then, but before she walked into the hotel, Jill turned back to see Jordan strolling in the opposite direction, away from her.

JILL AWOKE LATE the following morning. It was rare for her to sleep past eight-thirty, even on weekends. The tour bus wasn't scheduled to leave the hotel until ten, so she took her time showering and dressing. Breakfast consisted of coffee, an English muffin and slices of fresh pineapple, which she ate leisurely on her lanai, savoring the morning sunlight.

Out of curiosity, she glanced over at Jordan's room to see if the draperies were open. They were. From what she could discern, he was sitting at a table near the window, talking on his phone and working with his computer.

Business. Business. Business.

The man lived and breathed it, just the way her father had. And, in the end, it had killed him.

Dismissing Jordan from her thoughts, she reached for her purse and hurried down to the lobby where she was meeting the tour group.

The sight-seeing expedition proved excellent. Jill visited Pearl Harbor and the U.S.S. *Arizona* memorial and a huge shopping mall, returning to the hotel by three o'clock.

Her room was cool and inviting. Jill took a few minutes to examine the souvenirs she'd purchased, a shell lei and several colorful T-shirts. Then, with a good portion of the day still left to enjoy, she decided to spend the remaining afternoon hours lazing around the pool. Once again she glanced across the way to Jordan's room, her action almost involuntary. And once again she saw that he was on the phone. Jill wondered if he'd been talking since the morning.

Changing into her bathing suit, a modest one-piece in a—what else—Hawaiian print, she carried her beach bag, complete with three different kinds of tanning lotion, down to the swimming pool. With a large straw hat perched on her head and sunglasses protecting her eyes, she stretched out on a chaise longue to absorb the sun.

She hadn't been there more than fifteen minutes when a waiter approached carrying a dome-covered platter and a glass of champagne. "Ms. Morrison?"

"Yes?" Jill sat up abruptly, knocking her hat askew. "I . . . I didn't order anything," she said uncertainly as she reached up to straighten the hat.

"This was sent compliments of Mr. Wilcox."

"Oh." Jill wasn't sure what to say. She twisted around and, shading her eyes with her hand, looked up. Jordan was standing on his lanai. She waved, and he returned the gesture.

"If that will be all?" the waiter murmured, stepping away.

"Yes . . . Oh, just a moment." Jill scrambled in her beach bag for a tip, which she handed to the young man. He smiled his appreciation.

Curious, she balanced the glass of champagne as she lifted the lid—and nearly laughed out loud. Inside was a large array of crackers topped with caviar. She glanced up at Jordan a second time and blew him a kiss.

Something must have distracted him then. He turned away, and when Jill saw him again a few minutes later, he was pacing the lanai, phone in hand. She was convinced he'd completely forgotten about her. It was ironic, she mused, and really rather sad; here he was in paradise and he'd hardly ventured beyond his hotel room.

Jill drank her champagne and savored a few of the caviar-laden crackers, then decided she couldn't stand his attitude a minute longer. Packing up her things, she looped the towel around her neck and picked up the platter in one hand, her beach bag in the other. Then she headed back inside the hotel. She knew she was breaking her promise to herself by seeking him out, but she couldn't stop herself.

Muttering under her breath, she rode the elevator up to Jordan's floor, calculated which room was his and knocked boldly on the door.

A long moment passed before the door finally opened. Jordan, still talking on his phone, gestured her inside. He didn't so much as pause in his conversation, tossing dollar figures around as casually as other people talked about the weather.

Jill sat on the foot of his bed and crossed her legs, swinging her foot impatiently as Jordan strode back and forth across the carpet, seemingly oblivious to her presence.

"Listen, Rick, something's come up," he said, darting a look in her direction. "Give me a call in five minutes. Sure, sure, no problem. Five minutes. This shouldn't take any longer. See if you can contact Raymond, get these numbers to him, then call me back." He disconnected the line without a word of farewell, then glanced at Jill.

"Hello," he said.

"Hi," she returned, holding out the platter to offer him an hors d'oeuvre.

"No, thanks."

She took one herself and chewed it slowly. She could almost feel his irritation.

"Something I can do for you?"

"Yes," she stated calmly. "Sit down a minute."

"Sit down?"

She nodded, motioning toward the table. "I have a story to tell you."

"A story?" He didn't sound particularly charmed by the idea.

"Yes, and I promise it won't take longer than five minutes," she added pointedly.

He was obviously relieved that she intended to keep this short. "Go on."

"As I've mentioned before, I don't know a whole lot about the world of high finance. But I'm well aware that time has skyrocketed in value during the last fifteen or so years. I also realize that the value of any commodity depends on its availability.''

"Does this story have a point?"

"Actually I haven't got to the story yet, but I will soon," she announced cheerfully.

"Can you do it in—" he paused and glanced at his watch "—two and a half minutes?"

"I'll hurry," she promised, and drew a deep breath. "I was nine when my mother signed me up for piano lessons. I could hardly wait. The other kids dreaded having to practice, but not me. From the time I was in kindergarten, I loved to pound away at the old upright in our living room. My heart and soul went into making music. It was probably no coincidence that one of the first pieces I learned was 'Heart and Soul.' I hammered out those notes like machine-gun blasts. I overemphasized each crescendo, cherished each lingering note. Van Cliburn couldn't have finished a piece with more pizazz than I did. My hands would fly into the air, then flutter gently to my lap.''

"I noticed you standing by the piano at the dinner party. Are you a musician?"

"Nope. For all my theatrical talents, I had one serious shortcoming. I could never master the caesura—the rest.''

"The rest?"

"You know, that little zigzag thingamajig on sheet music that instructs the player to do nothing.''

"Nothing," he repeated slowly.

"My impatience was a disappointment to my mother. I'm sure I frustrated my piano teacher no end.

As hard as she tried, she couldn't make me understand that music was always sweeter and more compelling after a rest."

"I see." His hands were buried deep in his pockets
as he studied her.

If Jordan was as much like her father as she suspected, she doubted he really did understand. But
she'd told him what she'd come to say. Mission accomplished. There wasn't any other reason to stay, so
she got briskly to her feet and reached for her beach
bag.

"That's it?"

"That's it. Thank you for the caviar. It was a de-
lightful surprise." With that she moved toward his
door. "Just remember what I said about the rest," she
said, glancing over her shoulder.

The phone pealed sharply just then and Jill grimaced. "Goodbye," she mouthed, grasping the
doorknob.

The phone rang again. "Goodbye." Jordan hesitated. "Jill?"

"Yes?" The way he said her name seemed so urgent. She whirled around, hope surging in her heart.
Perhaps he didn't intend to answer the ring!

The phone went a third time, and Jordan's eyes,
dark gray, smoky with indecision, traveled from Jill to
the telephone.

"Yes?" she repeated.

"Nothing," he said harshly, reaching for the phone.
"Thanks for the story."

"You're welcome." With nothing left to say, Jill walked out of his room and closed the door. Even before the lock slid into place she heard Jordan rhyming off lists of figures.

Her room felt less welcoming than when she'd returned earlier. Jill slipped out of her swimsuit and showered. She was vain enough to check her reflection in the mirror, hoping to have enhanced the slight tan she'd managed to achieve between Seattle's infamous June cloudbursts. It didn't look as though her sojourn in the tropics had done anything but add a not-so-fetching touch of pink across her shoulders.

She dressed in a thick terry robe supplied by the hotel and had just wrapped a towel around her wet hair when her phone rang.

"Hello," she said, breathlessly, sinking onto her bed. Her stomach knotted with anticipation.

"Jill Morrison?"

"Yes." It wasn't Jordan. But the voice sounded vaguely familiar, though she couldn't immediately place it.

"Andrew Howard. I sat next to you at the dinner party last night."

"Yes, of course." Her voice rose with delight. She'd thoroughly enjoyed her chat with the older man. "How are you?"

He chuckled. "Just fine. I tried to phone earlier, but you were out."

"I went on a tour first thing this morning."

"Ah, that explains it. I realize it's rather short notice, but would you be free for dinner tonight?"

Jill didn't hesitate. "Yes, I am."

"Good, good. Could you join me around eight?"

"Eight would be perfect." Normally Jill dined much earlier, but she wasn't hungry yet, thanks to an expensive snack, compliments of Jordan Wilcox.

"Wonderful." Mr. Howard seemed genuinely pleased. "I'll have a car waiting for you and Wilcox out front at seven-thirty."

And Wilcox. She'd almost missed the words. So Jordan had accepted Mr. Howard's invitation. Perhaps she'd been too critical; perhaps he'd understood the point of her story, after all, and was willing to put business aside for one evening. Perhaps he was as eager to spend time with her as she was with him.

"I WONDERED if you'd be here," Jordan announced when they met in the lobby at the appointed time. He didn't exactly greet her with open enthusiasm, but Jill comforted herself with the observation that Jordan wasn't one to reveal his emotions.

"I wouldn't miss this for the world," he added. That was when she remembered he was hoping to have the older man invest in his shopping-mall project. Dinner, for Jordan, would be a golden opportunity to conduct business, elicit Mr. Howard's support and gain the financial backing he needed for the project.

Realizing all this, Jill couldn't help feeling disappointed. "I'll do my best not to interrupt your sales pitch," she said, a little sarcastically.

"My sales pitch?" he echoed, then grinned, apparently amused by her assumption. "You don't have to worry. Howard doesn't want in on this project, which is fine. He just likes to keep tabs on me, especially since Dad died. He seems to think I need a mentor, or at least some kind of paternal adviser.''

"Do you?''

Jordan hesitated. ''There've been one or two occasions when I've appreciated his wisdom. I don't need him holding my hand, but I have sometimes looked to him for advice.''

Remembering her dinner conversation with the older man, Jill said, ''In some ways, Mr. Howard must think of you as a son.''

Jordan shrugged. ''I doubt that.'' Then he scowled, muttering, ''I've known him all this time and not once did he ever mention he'd lost a son.''

''It was almost thirty years ago, and as I told you, it's the reason his company's done so much cancer research. Howard Pharmaceuticals makes several of the leading cancer-fighting medications.'' When Andrew Howard had told her about his son's death, a tear had come to his eye. Although Jeff Howard had succumbed to childhood leukemia a long time ago, his father still grieved. Andrew had become a widower a few years later, and he'd never fully recovered from the double blow. Jill was deeply touched by Mr. Howard's story. During their conversation, she'd shared a little of the pain she had felt at her own father's death, something she rarely did, even with her mother or her closest friend.

''What amazes me,'' Jordan continued, ''is that I've worked on different projects with him over the years. We've also kept in touch socially. And not once, *not once,* did he mention a son.''

"Perhaps there was never a reason.''

Jordan dismissed that idea with a shake of his head.

"Mr. Howard's a sweet man. I couldn't help liking him,'' Jill asserted.

"Sweet? Andrew Howard?'' Jordan grinned, his eyes bright with humor. "I've known alligators with more agreeable personalities.''

"Apparently there's more to your friend than you realized.''

"My friend,'' Jordan repeated. "Funny, I'd always thought of him as my father's friend, not my own. But you're right—he *is* my friend and— Oh, here's the car.'' With a hand on her arm, he escorted her outside.

A tall, uniformed driver stepped from the long white limousine. "Ms. Morrison and Mr. Wilcox?'' he asked crisply.

Jordan nodded, and the chauffeur ceremoniously opened the back door for them. Soon they were heading out of the city toward the island's opposite coast.

"Do you still play the piano?'' Jordan asked unexpectedly.

"Every so often, when the mood strikes me,'' Jill told him a bit ruefully. "Not as much as I'd like.''

"I take it you still haven't conquered the caesura?''

"Not yet, but I'm learning.'' She wasn't sure what had prompted his question, then decided to ask a few of her own. "What about you? Do you think you might be interested in learning to play the piano?''

Jordan shook his head adamantly. "Unfortunately, I've never had much interest in that sort of thing."

Jill sighed and looked away.

Nearly thirty minutes passed before they reached Andrew Howard's oceanside estate. Jill suspected it was the longest Jordan had gone without a business conversation since he'd registered at the hotel.

Her heart pounded as they approached the beautifully landscaped grounds. A security guard pushed a button that opened a huge wrought-iron gate. They drove down a private road, nearly a mile long and bordered on each side by rolling green lawns and tropical-flower beds. At the end stood a sprawling stone house.

No sooner had the car stopped when Mr. Howard hurried out of the house, grinning broadly.

"Welcome, welcome!" He greeted them expansively, holding out his arms to Jill.

In a spontaneous display of affection, she hugged him and kissed his cheek. "Thank you so much for inviting us."

"The pleasure's all mine. Come inside. Everything's ready and waiting." After a hearty handshake with Jordan, Mr. Howard led the way into his home.

Jill had been impressed with the outside, but the beauty of the interior overwhelmed her. The entryway was tiled in white marble and illuminated by a sparkling crystal chandelier. Huge crystal vases of vivid pink and purple hibiscus added color and life. From there, Mr. Howard escorted them into a massive living room with floor-to-ceiling windows that overlooked the Pacific. Frothing waves crashed against the shore, bathed in the fire of an island sunset.

"This is lovely," Jill breathed in awe.

"I knew you'd appreciate it." Mr. Howard reached for a bell, which he rang once. Almost immediately the housekeeper appeared, carrying a tray of glasses and bottles of white and red wine, sherry and assorted aperitifs.

They were sipping their drinks when the same woman reappeared. "Mr. Wilcox, there's a phone call for you."

It was all Jill could do not to gnash her teeth. The man was never free, the phone cord wrapped around his neck tighter than a hangman's noose.

"Excuse me, please," Jordan said as he left the room, his step brisk.

Jill looked away, refusing to watch him go.

"How do you feel about that young man?" Mr. Howard asked bluntly when Jordan was gone.

"We met only recently. I—I don't have any feelings for him one way or the other."

"Well, then, what do you think of him?"

Jill's gaze remained stubbornly focused on her wine. "He works too hard."

Sighing, the old man nodded and rubbed his eyes. "He reminds me of myself more than thirty years ago. Sometimes I'd like to take him by the shoulders and shake some sense into him, but I doubt it'd do much good. That boy's too stubborn to listen. Unfortunately, he's a lot like his father.''

Knowing so little of Jordan and his background, Jill was eager to learn what she could. At the same time, a saner part of her insisted she was better off not hearing this. The more she knew, the greater her chances were of caring.

Nevertheless, Jill found herself asking curiously, ''What made Jordan the way he is?''

''To begin with, his parents divorced when he was young. It was a sad situation.'' Andrew leaned forward and clasped his wineglass with both hands. ''It was plain as the nose on your face that James and Gladys Wilcox were in love. But, somehow, bitterness replaced the love, and their son became a weapon they used against each other.''

''Oh, how sad.'' Just as she'd feared, Jill felt herself sympathizing with Jordan.

''They both married other people, and Jordan seemed to remind his parents of their earlier unhappiness. He was sent to the best boarding schools, but there was precious little love in his life. Before he died, James tried to build a relationship with his son, but...'' He shrugged. ''And to the best of my knowledge his mother hasn't seen him since he was a teenager. I'm afraid he's had very little experience of real love, the kind that gives life meaning. Oh, there've been women, plenty of them, but never one who could teach him how to love and bring joy into his life—until now.'' He paused and looked pointedly at Jill.

"As I said before, I've only known Jordan a short while."

"Be patient with him," Mr. Howard continued as though Jill hadn't spoken. "Jordan's talented, don't get me wrong—the boy's got a way of pulling a deal together that amazes just about everyone—but there are times when he seems to forget about human values, like compassion. And the ability to enjoy what you have."

Jill wasn't sure how to respond.

"Frankly, I was beginning to lose faith in him," Mr. Howard said, grinning sheepishly. "He can be hard and unforgiving. You've given me the first ray of hope."

Jill took a big swallow of wine.

"He needs you. Your warmth, your gentleness, your love."

Jill wanted to weep with frustration. Mr. Howard was telling her exactly what she didn't want to hear. "I'm sure you're mistaken," she mumbled.

Mr. Howard chuckled. "I doubt that, but I'm an old man, so indulge me, will you?"

"Of course, but—"

"There's a reason you've come into his life," he said, gazing intently at her. "A very important reason." Andrew closed his eyes. "I feel this more profoundly than I've felt anything in a long while. He needs you, Jill."

"No...I'm sure he doesn't." Jill realized she was beginning to sound desperate, but she couldn't help it.

The old man's eyes opened slowly and he smiled. "And I'm just as sure he does." He would have continued, but Jordan returned to the room then.

From the marinated-shrimp appetizer to the homemade mango-and-pineapple ice cream, dinner was one of the most delectable, elegant meals Jill had ever tasted. They lingered over coffee, followed by a glass of smooth brandy. By the end of the evening, Jill felt mellow and warm, a dangerous sensation. Jordan had been wonderful company—witty, charming, fun. He seemed more relaxed, too. Apparently the phone call had brought good news; it was the only thing to which she could attribute his cheerfulness.

"I can't thank you enough," she told Andrew when the limousine arrived to drive her and Jordan back to the hotel. "I can't remember a lovelier evening."

"The pleasure was all mine." The older man hugged Jill and whispered close to her ear, "Remember what I said." Breaking away, he extended his hand, gripping Jordan's elbow as the two exchanged meaningful looks. "It was good of you to come."

"I'll be in touch again soon," Jordan promised.

"Good, good. I'll look forward to hearing from you. Let me know what happens with this shopping-mall project."

"I will," Jordan promised.

The car was cool and inviting in the warm night. Before she realized it, Jill found her head resting on Jordan's broad shoulder. "Oh, sorry," she mumbled through a yawn.

"Are you sleepy?"

She smiled softly to herself, too tired to fight the powers of attraction—and exhaustion. "Maybe a little. Wine makes me sleepy."

Jordan pressed her head against his shoulder and held her there. His hand gently stroked her hair. "Do you mind telling me what went on between you and Howard while I was on the phone?"

Jill went stock-still. "Uh, nothing. What makes you ask?" She decided it was best to pretend she didn't know what he was talking about.

"Then why was Howard wearing a silly grin every time he looked at me?" Jordan demanded.

"I—I don't know, you'll have to ask him." She tried to straighten up, but Jordan wouldn't allow it. After a moment she gave up, too relaxed to put up much of a struggle.

"I swear there was a twinkle in his eye from the moment I returned from the telephone call. It was like I'd been left out of a joke."

"I'm sure you're wrong."

Jordan seemed to ponder that. "I don't think so."

"Hmm." She felt sleepy, and leaning against Jordan was strangely comforting.

"I've been thinking about what you said this afternoon," he told her a few minutes later. His mouth was against her ear, and although she might have been mistaken, she thought his lips lightly brushed her cheek.

"My sad but true tale," she whispered on the end of a yawn.

"About your trouble with the musical rest."

"Ah, yes, the rest."

"I'm flying back to Seattle tomorrow," Jordan said abruptly.

Jill nodded, feeling inexplicably sad, then surprised by the intensity of her reaction. With Jordan in Seattle, they wouldn't be bumping into each other at every turn. Wouldn't be arguing, bantering—or kissing. With Jordan in Seattle, she wouldn't confuse him with the legacy behind Aunt Milly's wedding dress. "Well . . . I hope you have a good flight."

"I have a meeting Tuesday morning. It would be impossible to cancel at this late date, but I was able to change my flight."

"You changed your flight?" Jill prayed he wouldn't hear the breathless catch in her voice.

"I don't have to be at the airport until early evening."

"How early?" It shouldn't make any difference to her, yet she found herself wanting to know. Needing to know.

"Eight."

Jill was much too dazed to calculate the time difference, but she knew it meant he'd arrive in Seattle sometime in the early morning. He'd be exhausted. Not exactly the best way to arrive at a high-powered meeting.

"I was thinking," Jordan continued. "I've been to Hawaii a number of times but other than meetings or dinner engagements, I haven't seen much of the islands. I've never explored them."

"That's a pity," she said, meaning it.

"And," he went on, "it seemed to me that sight-seeing wouldn't be nearly as much fun alone."

"I enjoyed myself this morning." Her effort to refute him was weak at best.

His fingers were entwined in her hair. "Will you come with me, Jill?" he asked, his voice a husky murmur. "Share the day with me. Let's discover Hawaii together."

CHAPTER FOUR

"I CAN'T," was Jill's immediate response. She'd already lowered her guard—enough to be snuggling in his arms. So much for her resolve not to become involved with Jordan Wilcox, she thought with dismay. So much for steering a wide course around the man.

"Why not?" Jordan asked with the directness she'd come to expect from him.

"I've...already made plans," she stammered. Even now, she could feel herself weakening. With his arm tucked around her and her head nestled against his shoulder it was difficult to refuse him.

"Cancel them."

How arrogant of him to assume she should abandon her plans because the almighty businessman was willing to grant her some of his valuable time.

"I'm afraid I can't do that," she answered coolly, her determination reinforced. She'd already paid for the rental car as part of her vacation package, she rationalized, and she wasn't about to let that money go to waste.

"Why not?" He sounded surprised.

Isn't spending time with him what you really want? The question stole into her mind, and Jill wanted to scream out her response. A resounding NO. Jordan Wilcox frightened her. It was all too easy to envision them together, strolling hand in hand along sun-drenched beaches. He'd kissed her that first time, that only time, on the beach, and the memory stubbornly refused to go away.

"Jill?"

At the softness in his voice, she involuntarily raised her gaze to his. Their eyes held for the longest time. Jill hadn't expected ever to see tenderness in Jordan, but she did now, and it was nearly her undoing. Her feelings for him were changing, and she found herself more strongly attracted than ever. She remembered the first time she'd seen him, the way she'd been convinced there was nothing gentle in him. He'd seemed so hard, so untouchable. Yet now, this very moment, he'd made himself vulnerable to her. For her.

"You're trembling," he said, running his hands down the length of her arm. "What's wrong?"

"Nothing," she denied quickly, breathlessly. "I'm . . . a little tired, I guess. It's been a long day."

"That's what you said last night when I kissed you. Remember? You started mumbling some nonsense about a dress, then you went stiff as a board on me."

"Nothing's wrong," she insisted, breaking away from him. She straightened and lowered her hand to her skirt, smoothing away imaginary creases.

"I don't buy that, Jill. Something's bothering you."

She wished he hadn't mentioned the dress, because it brought to mind, uninvited and unwanted, Aunt

Milly's wedding dress, which was hanging in her hotel-room closet.

"You'd be shaking, too, if you knew the things I did," she exclaimed, instantly regretting the impulse.

"You're afraid of something?"

She stared out the window, then slowly her lower lip began to tremble with the effort to restrain her laughter. She was actually frightened of a silly dress! She wasn't afraid to fall in love; she just didn't want it to be with Jordan.

"For a woman who drags a wedding dress on vacation with her, you're not doing very much to encourage romance."

"I did not bring that dress with me."

"It was in the room when you arrived? Someone left it behind?"

"Not exactly. My friend Shelly, uh, enjoys a good laugh. She mailed it to me."

"It never occurred to me that you might be engaged," he said slowly. "You're not, are you?"

"No." But according to her best friend, she soon would be.

"Who's Shelly?"

"My best friend," Jill explained, "or at least she used to be." Then, impulsively, her heart racing, she added, "Listen, Jordan, I think you have a lot of potential in the husband category, but I can't fall in love with you. I just can't."

A stunned silence followed her announcement.

He cocked his eyebrows. "Aren't you taking a few things for granted here? I asked you to explore the island with me, not bear my children."

She'd done it again, blurted out something totally illogical. Worse, she couldn't make herself stop. Children were a subject near and dear to her heart.

"That's another thing," she wailed. "I bet you don't even like children. No, I just can't go with you tomorrow. Please don't ask me to... because it's so hard to say no." It must be the wine, Jill decided; she was telling him far more than she should.

Jordan relaxed against the leather upholstery and crossed his long legs. "All right, if you'd rather not go, I'm certainly not going to force you."

His easy acceptance astonished her. She glanced at him out of the corner of her eye, feeling almost disappointed that he wasn't trying to convince her.

Something was drastically, dangerously, wrong with her. She was beginning to like Jordan, really like him. Yet she couldn't allow this attraction to continue. She couldn't allow herself to fall in love with a man so much like her father. Because she knew what that meant, what kind of life it led to, what kind of unhappiness it engendered.

When the limousine stopped in front of the hotel, it was all Jill could do to wait for the chauffeur to climb out of the driver's seat, walk around and open the door for her.

She didn't wait for Jordan, but hurried inside the lobby, needing to breathe in the fresh air of reason. Wait for sanity to catch up with her heart.

She paused in front of the elevators and pushed the button, holding her thumb against the plate, hoping that would hurry it along.

"Next time, keep your little anecdotes to yourself," Jordan said sharply from behind her, then walked leisurely across the lobby.

Keep her little anecdotes to herself? The temptation to rush after him and demand an explanation was strong, but Jill forced herself to resist it.

Not until she was in the elevator did she understand. This entire discussion had arisen because she'd told him her story about the caesura and her lack of real musical talent. And now he was turning her own disclosure against her! She allowed the righteous anger to build in her heart.

But by the time Jill was in her room and ready for bed, she felt wretched. Jordan had asked her to spend a day with him, and she'd reacted as if he'd insulted her.

The way she'd gone on and on about his potential as a husband was bad enough, but then she'd dragged the subject of children into their conversation. That mortified her even more. The wine could be blamed for only so much.

She cringed, too, as she recalled what Andrew Howard had said, the faith he'd placed in her. Jordan needed her, he'd insisted, apparently convinced that Jordan would never know love if she didn't teach him. She hated the thought of disappointing Andrew Howard, and yet ... and yet ...

It didn't surprise Jill that she slept poorly. By morning she wasn't feeling the least bit enthusiastic about picking up her rental car or viewing the sights on the north shore.

She reviewed the room-service menu, ordered coffee and toast, then stared at the phone for several minutes before conceding there was one thing she still had to do. Anxious to get it over with, Jill rang through to Jordan's room.

"Hello," he answered gruffly on the first ring. He was definitely a man who never ventured far from his phone.

"Hello," she said with uncharacteristic meekness. "I'm ... calling to apologize."

"Are you sorry enough to change your mind and spend the day with me?"

Jill hesitated. "I've already paid for a rental car."

"Great, then I won't need to order one."

Jill closed her eyes. She knew what she was going to say, had known it the night before. In the same heartbeat, she realized she'd regret it later. "Yes," she whispered. "If you still want me to join you, I'll meet you in the lobby in half an hour."

"Twenty minutes."

She groaned. "Fine, twenty minutes, then."

Despite her misgivings, Jill's spirits lifted immediately. "One day won't hurt anything," she said bracingly to herself. What could possibly happen in so short a time? Certainly nothing earth-shattering. Nothing of consequence.

Who was she kidding? Not herself, Jill admitted.

She thought she understood why a moth ventured close to the fire, enticed by the light and the warmth. Against her will, Jordan was drawing her dangerously close to him. She knew even as she came nearer that she'd walk away burned. And yet she didn't hesitate.

He was waiting for her when she stepped out of the elevator and into the lobby. He stood, grinning, his look almost boyish. This was the first time she'd seen him without a business suit. Instead, he wore white slacks and a pale blue shirt, with the sleeves rolled up.

"You ready?" he asked, taking her beach bag from her.

"One question first." Her heart was pounding because she had no right to ask.

"Sure." His eyes held hers.

"Your portable phone—is it in the hotel room?" Jordan nodded.

"What about your pager?"

He pulled an impossibly tiny device from his shirt pocket. Jill stared at it for several moments, feeling the tension work its way down her neck and back. Her father had always carried a pager. All family outings, which were few and far between, had been subject to outside interference. Early in life, Jill had received a clear message: business was more important to her father than she was. In fact, almost everything had seemed more significant than spending time with those who'd loved him.

Jordan must have read the look in her eyes because he said, "I'll leave it at the front desk," and then promptly did so. Stunned, Jill watched as he handed it to the hotel clerk. Bit by bit, her muscles began to relax.

While he was busy at the hotel desk, Jill filled out the necessary paperwork for the rental car. She was waiting outside by the economy model when Jordan appeared. He paused, staring at the vehicle with narrowed eyes as if he wasn't sure it would make it to the end of the street, let alone around the island.

"I'm on a limited budget," Jill explained, hiding a smile. The car suited her petite frame perfectly, but for a man of Jordan's stature it was a little like stuffing a rag doll inside a pickle jar, Jill thought, enjoying the whimsical comparison.

"You're sure this thing runs?" he muttered under his breath as he climbed into the driver's seat. His long legs were cramped below the steering wheel, his head practically touching the roof.

"Relatively sure." Jill remembered reading that this particular model got exceptionally good gas mileage—but then it should, with an engine only a little bigger than a lawnmower's.

To prove her right, the car roared to life with a flick of the key.

"Where are we headed?" Jill asked once they'd merged with the flow of traffic on the busy thoroughfare by the hotel.

"The airport."

"The airport?" she repeated, struggling to hide her disappointment. "I thought your flight didn't leave until eight."

"Mine doesn't, but ours takes off in half an hour."

"Ours?" What about the sugarcane fields and watching the workers harvest pineapple? Surely he didn't intend for them to miss that. "Where is this plane taking us?"

"Hawaii," he announced casually. "The island of. Do you know how to scuba dive?"

"No." Her voice was oddly breathless and high-pitched. She might have spent the past twenty-odd years in Seattle—practically surrounded by water—but she wasn't all that comfortable *under* it.

"How about snorkeling?"

"Ah..." She jerked her thumb over her shoulder. "There are pineapple fields on the other side of this island. I thought you'd want to see those."

"Another time, perhaps. I'd like to try my hand at marlin fishing, but we don't have enough time today."

"Snorkeling," Jill said as though she'd never heard the word before. "Well...it might be fun." In her guidebook Jill remembered reading about green beaches of crushed olivine crystals and black sands of soft lava. These were sights she couldn't expect to find anywhere else. However, she wasn't entirely convinced she wanted to view them through a rubber mask!

A small private plane was ready for them when they arrived at Honolulu Airport. The pilot, who apparently knew Jordan, greeted them cordially. After brief introductions and a few minutes' chat, they were on their way.

Another car, considerably larger than the one Jill had rented, was waiting for them on the island of Hawaii. A large, white wicker picnic basket sat in the middle of the back seat.

"I hope you're hungry."

"Not yet."

"You will be," Jordan promised.

He drove for perhaps half an hour until they reached a deserted inlet with a magnificent waterfall. He parked the car, then got out and opened the trunk. Inside was everything they'd need for snorkeling in the crystal-clear aquamarine waters.

Never having done this before, Jill was uncertain of the procedure. Jordan patiently answered her questions and waded into the water with her. He paused when they were waist-deep, gave her detailed instructions, then clasped her hand. Being linked with him lent her confidence, and soon she was investigating an undersea world of breathtaking beauty. Swimming out of the inlet, they happened upon a reef, with colorful fish slipping in and out of white coral caverns. After what seemed like only minutes, Jordan steered them back toward the inlet and shore.

"I don't think I've ever seen anything more beautiful," she breathed, pushing the mask from her face.

"I don't think I have, either," he agreed as they stepped out of the water.

While Jill ran a comb through her hair and put on a shirt to protect her shoulders from the sun, Jordan brought out their lunch.

He spread the blanket in the shade of a palm tree. Jill joined him there, kneeling down to open the basket. Inside were generous crab-salad sandwiches, fresh slices of papaya and pineapple and thick chocolate-chip cookies. She removed two cold cans of soda and handed one to Jordan.

They ate, then napped with a cool, gentle breeze whisking over them.

Jill awoke before Jordan. He was asleep on his back with his hand thrown carelessly across his face, shading his eyes from the glare of the sun. His features were more relaxed than she'd ever seen them. Jill studied him for several moments, her heart aching for the man she'd loved so much, so long ago. Her father. The man she'd never really had the chance to know. In certain ways, Jordan was so much like her father it pained her to be with him, and at the same time it thrilled her. Not only because in learning about Jordan she was discovering a part of her past, of herself, she'd assumed was gone, but because she'd rarely felt so *alive* in anyone's company.

As she recognized this truth, a heaviness settled on her heart. She didn't want to fall in love with him. She was so afraid her life would mirror her mother's. Elaine Morrison had grown embittered. She'd been a young woman when her husband died, but she'd never remarried; instead she'd closed off her heart, not wanting to risk again the pain that loving Jill's father had brought her.

Sitting up, Jill brushed her now-dry hair from her face. She wrapped her arms around her bent legs and pressed her forehead to her knees, gulping in breath after breath.

"Jill?" His voice was soft, husky. Gentle.

"You shouldn't have left your pager behind, after all," she told him, her voice tight. "Or your phone." Without them, he was a handsome, compelling man who appealed to all her senses. Without them, she was defenseless against his charm.

"Why not?"

"Because I like you too much."

"That's a problem?"

"Yes!" she cried. "Don't you understand?"

"Obviously not," he said with such tenderness she wanted to vault to her feet and yell at him to stop. "Maybe you'd better explain it to me," he added.

"I can't," she whispered, keeping her head lowered. "You'd never believe me. I don't blame you—I wouldn't believe me, either."

Jordan hesitated. "Does this have something to do with your reaction the first time I kissed you?"

"The only time!"

"That's about to change."

Her head shot up at the casual way in which he said it, as though kissing her was a foregone conclusion.

He was right.

His kiss was gentle. Jill resisted, unwilling to grant him her heart, knowing what became of women who loved men like this. Men like Jordan Wilcox.

It happened again, only now it was much more potent than that first night. His touch somehow transcended the sensual. Jill could think of no other way to describe it. His fingers brushed her temple. His lips moved across her face, grazing her chin, her cheek, her eyes. She moaned, not from pleasure, but from fear, from a pain that reached deep inside her.

"Oh, no..."

"It's happening again, isn't it?" he whispered.

She nodded. "Can you feel it?"

"Yes. I did the first time, too."

Her eyes drifted slowly open. "I can't love you."

"So you've told me. More than once."

"It isn't anything personal." She tried to break free without being obvious about it, but Jordan held her firmly in his embrace.

"Tell me what's upsetting you so much."

"I can't." Looking into the distance, she focused on the smoky-blue outline of a mountain. Anything to keep her gaze away from Jordan.

"You're involved with someone else, aren't you?"

It would be so easy to lie to him. To tell him about Ralph as though the friendship they shared was one of blazing passion, but she found she couldn't make herself do it.

"No," she wailed, "but I wish I was."

"Why?" he demanded gruffly.

"What about you?" she countered with a question of her own. "Why did you seek out my company? Why'd you ask me to attend the dinner party with you? Surely there was someone else, someone far more suitable."

"I'll admit no other woman reacts to my kisses the way you do," he confessed.

"But I've been rude."

"Actually, more amusing than rude."

"But why?" she asked. "What is it about me that interests you? We're about as different as two people can get. We're strangers—strangers with nothing in common."

Jordan was frowning, his eyes revealing his own lack of understanding. "I don't know."

"See what I mean?" She spoke as if it were the jury's final decree. "The whole thing is a farce. You kiss me and...and I feel a certain...feeling."

"Feeling? Is that all you can say about it? Sweetheart, I've seen electrical storms unleash less energy than when I take you in my arms."

Suddenly Jill found it nearly impossible to breathe. Jordan couldn't possibly be affected by the wedding dress and its so-called magic—could he? Jill swore the minute she arrived in Seattle she was returning it to Shelly and Mark. She wasn't taking any chances!

"You remind me of my father," Jill said, refusing to meet his eyes. Even talking about Adam Morrison produced a pain in her heart. "He was always in a hurry to get somewhere, to meet someone, to make a deal. We took a family vacation when I was ten. We saw California in one day, Disneyland in an hour. Do you get the picture?" She didn't wait for a response. "He died of a heart attack when I was fifteen. We were wealthy by a lot of people's standards, and after his death my mother didn't have to work. There was even a fund set aside for my college expenses."

An awkward moment passed. When Jordan didn't comment, Jill glanced at him. "You don't have anything to say?"

"Not really, other than to remind you I'm not your father."

"But in a way you are. I recognized it the first minute I saw you." She leapt to her feet, grabbed her towel and crammed it into her beach bag.

Jordan reluctantly stood, and while she shook the sand off the blanket and folded it, he loaded their snorkeling gear into the trunk of the car.

They were both quiet during the drive back to the airport, the silence strained and unnatural. A couple of times, Jill glanced in Jordan's direction. The hardness was back. The tightness in his jaw, the harsh, almost grim expression . . .

Jill could well imagine what he'd be like in a board meeting. No wonder he didn't seem too concerned about the threat of a takeover. He would withstand that, and a whole lot more, in the years to come. But at what price? Power demanded sacrifice; prestige didn't come cheap. There was a cost, and Jill could only speculate what it would be for Jordan. His health? His happiness?

She found it intolerable to think about. Words burned on her heart. Words of caution. Words of appeal, but he wouldn't listen to her any more than her father had heeded the tearful pleas of her mother.

As the airport came into view, Jill knew she couldn't let their day end on such an unhappy note. "I did have a wonderful time. Thank you."

"Mmm," he replied, his gaze focused on the road ahead.

Jill stared at him. "Is that all you can say?"

"What do you want me to say?" His voice was crisp and emotionless.

"Like, I don't know, that you enjoyed yourself, too."

"It was interesting."

"Interesting?" Jill repeated.

They'd had a marvelous adventure! Not only that, he'd actually *relaxed.* The lines of fatigue around his eyes were gone. She'd bet a year's wages this was the first afternoon nap he'd had in years. Possibly decades. It was probably the longest stretch of time he'd been away from a telephone in his adult life.

All he'd admit was that their day had been "interesting"?

"What about the kissing?" she demanded, "was *that* interesting?"

"Very."

Jill seethed silently. "It was . . . interesting for me, too."

"So you claimed."

Jill tucked a long strand of hair behind her ear. "I was only being honest with you."

"I admit it was a fresh approach. Do you generally discuss marriage and children with a man on a first date?"

Color exploded in her cheeks, and she looked uncomfortably away. "No, but you were different . . . and it wasn't an approach."

"Excuse me, that's right, you were being honest." The cold sarcasm in his voice kept her from even trying to explain.

They'd almost reached the airport when she spoke again. "Would you do one small favor for me?" She nearly choked on the pride she had to swallow, hating to ask him for anything.

"What?"

"Would you... The next time you see Mr. Howard, would you tell him something for me? Would you tell him I'm sorry?" He'd be disappointed in her, but Jill couldn't risk her own happiness because a dear man with a romantic heart believed she was Jordan Wilcox's one chance at finding love.

Jordan hesitated, then stopped the car abruptly and turned to glare at her. "You want me to apologize to Howard?"

"Please."

"Sorry," he said without a pause. "You'll have to do that yourself."

CHAPTER FIVE

FOUR DAYS LATER, Jill stepped off the plane at Sea-Tac Airport in Seattle. Her skin glowed with a golden tan, accentuated by the bold pink-flower print of her slacks and matching blouse. She hadn't expected anyone to meet her, but was pleasantly surprised to see Shelly and Mark. Shelly waved excitedly when she located Jill.

"Welcome home," Shelly said as she rushed forward, exuberantly throwing her arms around Jill. "How was Hawaii? My goodness, your tan is gorgeous. You must have spent hours in the sun."

"Hawaii was wonderful." A slight exaggeration. She'd hardly slept since Jordan's departure.

"Tell me everything," Shelly insisted, gripping Jill's hands. "I'm dying to find out who you met after we mailed you the wedding dress."

"Honey," Mark chided gently, "give her a chance to breathe."

"Are you with someone?" Shelly asked, looking around expectantly. "I mean, you know, you're not married, are you?"

"I'm not even close to being married," Jill informed her friend dryly.

Mark collected the large beach bag Jill had brought home with her, stuffed full of souvenirs and everything else she couldn't fit inside her suitcase. She removed one of the three leis she was wearing and looped it around Shelly's neck. "Here, my gift to you."

"Oh, Jill, it's beautiful. Thank you," Shelly said, fingering the fragrant lei made of pink orchids. They were walking toward the baggage-claim area, and Shelly slipped her arm through Jill's. "I don't think I can wait a moment longer. Tell me what happened after the dress arrived. I want to hear every detail."

Jill had been dreading this moment, but she hadn't expected to face it quite so soon. "I'm afraid I'm going to have to return the dress."

Shelly stared at her as if she hadn't heard correctly. "I beg your pardon?"

"I didn't meet anyone."

"You mean to tell me you spent seven days in Hawaii and you didn't speak to a single man?" Shelly asked incredulously.

"Not exactly."

"Aha! So there was someone."

Jill swallowed a groan. "Sort of."

Shelly smiled, sliding one arm around her husband's waist. "The plot thickens."

"I met him briefly the first day. Actually I don't think he counts...."

"Why shouldn't he count?" Shelly demanded.

"We sat next to each other on the plane, so technically we met *before* I got the wedding dress, so I'm

sure he's not the one." Jill had decided to play along
with her friend's theory, pretend to take it more seriously than she actually did. Logical objections, like
this mistake in timing, should convince Shelly—but
probably wouldn't.

"In fact," she continued, "I've been thinking about
that dress lately, and I'm convinced you and your
Aunt Milly are wrong—it's not for me. It never was."

"But it fit you. Remember?"

Jill didn't need to be reminded. "That was a fluke.
I'm sure if I were to try it on now, it wouldn't."

"Then try it on! Prove me wrong."

"Here?" Jill laughed.

"When you get home. Anyway, never mind that
now. Just tell me about this guy you met. You keep
trying to avoid the subject."

"There's nothing to tell," Jill insisted, sorry she'd
said anything. She'd tried for the past few days to push
every thought of Jordan from her mind, with little
success. He'd haunted her remaining time on the islands, refusing to leave her alone. If she did sleep, he
invaded her dreams.

"Start with his name," Shelly said. "Surely you
know his name."

"Jordan Wilcox, but—"

"Jordan Wilcox," Mark repeated. "He doesn't
happen to be a developer, does he?"

"I think he does something along those lines."

Mark released a low whistle. "He's one of the big
boys."

"Big boys," Shelly echoed disparagingly. "Speak English. Do you mean he's tall?"

"No." Mark's smiling eyes briefly met Jill's. "He's a well-known corporate giant. I've met him a few times. If I understand it correctly, he puts together commercial projects, finds backers for them, works with the designer and the builders, and when the project's complete, he sells. He's made millions in the last few years. He's damn good at it."

"He was in Hawaii to put together financial backing for a shopping mall," Jill explained.

"Well," Shelly said, eyeing her closely, "what did you think of him?"

"What was there to think? I sat next to him on the plane and we stayed in the same hotel, but that was about it." It was best not to mention the other incidents; Shelly would put far too much stock in a couple of dinners and a day on the beach. Heaven help Jill if Shelly ever found out they'd exchanged a few kisses!

"I'm sure he's the one," Shelly announced gleefully. Her eyes fairly sparkled with delight. "I can *feel* it. He's our man."

"No, he isn't," Jill argued, knowing it was futile, yet compelled to try. "I already told you—I met him before the dress arrived. Besides, we have absolutely nothing in common."

"Do Mark and I?" Shelly glanced lovingly at her husband. "And I'm crazy about him."

At first, Jill had wondered what Mark, a tax consultant with orderly habits and a closetful of suits, could possibly have in common with her zany, creative, unconventional friend. The answer was simple. Nothing. But that hadn't stopped them from falling in love. Jill couldn't be in the same room with them without sensing the powerful attraction they felt for each other.

However, there was little similarity between Shelly's marriage to Mark and Jill's dealings with Jordan. Jill understood him; in many ways they were alike. But she'd learned from her father's life—and death—the value of bringing a balance into her life. Although her career mattered to her, it didn't define her life or occupy every minute of her time.

"In this case I think Jill might be right," Mark said, his voice low and thoughtful. "A man like Jordan Wilcox eats little girls like Jill for breakfast."

"He's the one," Shelly insisted for the second time.

"I've met the man," Mark went on to say. "He's cold and unemotional. If he does have a heart, it was frozen a long time ago."

"So?" Ever optimistic, Shelly refused to listen. "Jill's perfect for him, then. She's warm and gentle and caring."

Right now Jill didn't feel any of those things. Listening to Mark describe Jordan, she had to fight the urge to defend him, to tell them what Andrew Howard had told her. Yes, Jordan was everything Mark said, but there was another side to him, one Jill had briefly encountered. One that was so appealing it had frightened her into running away, which was exactly what she'd done that day on the beach. He'd kissed her and she'd known immediately, intuitively, that she'd never be the same. But knowing it didn't alter her resolve. She couldn't love him because the price would be too high. He would give her all the things she craved, a husband and family, wealth beyond her imagination. But eventually she'd end up like her mother, lonely and bitter.

"I just can't imagine Jordan Wilcox married," Mark concluded.

"I can," Shelly interrupted with unflinching enthusiasm. "To Jill."

"Shelly," Mark said, grinning indulgently, "listen to reason."

"When has falling in love ever been reasonable?" She fired the question at her husband, who merely shrugged, then turned back to Jill. "Did you tell him about Aunt Milly's wedding dress?"

"Good heavens, no!"

"All the better. I'll bet you really threw the guy for a loop. Was he on this flight?"

"No, he returned four days ago."

"Four days ago," Shelly echoed slowly, suspiciously. "There's something you're not telling us. Come on, Jill, 'fess up. You did a whole lot more than sit next to this guy on the plane. And Mark and I want to know what."

"Uh..." Jill was tired from the flight and her resistance was low. Under normal circumstances she would have sidestepped the issue. "It isn't the way it sounds," she said weakly. "We talked a couple of times, that's all."

"Did you kiss?" The question came out in a soft whisper. "The first time Mark kissed me was when I knew. If you and Jordan kissed, there wouldn't be any doubt in your mind. You'd know."

Sooner or later Shelly would worm it out of her. By telling the truth now, Jill thought she might be able to avoid a lengthy inquisition later. "All right, if you insist—yes, we did kiss. A couple of times."

Even Mark seemed surprised by that.

"See?" Shelly cried triumphantly. "And what happened?"

Jill heaved an exaggerated sigh. "Nothing. I want to return the wedding dress."

"Sorry," Shelly said, her eyes flashing with excitement, "it's nonreturnable."

"I don't plan on ever seeing him again," Jill said adamantly. She'd more or less told Jordan that, too. He was in full agreement; he wanted nothing to do with her, either. "I insist you take back the wedding dress," Jill repeated. Shelly and Mark's eyes met. Slowly they smiled, as if sharing a private joke.

But Jill wasn't laughing.

THE FIRST PERSON Jill called when she got home was her mother. Their conversation was friendly, and she was relieved to find her mother less vague and self-absorbed than she'd been recently. Jill shared a few anecdotes, described the island and the hotel, but resisted telling her mother about meeting Jordan.

She was strangely reluctant to call Ralph, even though she knew he was waiting to hear from her. He was terribly nice, but unfortunately she found him...a bit dull. She put off calling; two days later, he called her, leaving a message on her answering machine.

They'd kissed a few times, and the kisses were pleasant enough, but for her there wasn't any spark. When Jordan took her in his arms it felt like a forest fire compared to the placid warmth she experienced with Ralph.

Jordan. Forgetting him hadn't become any easier. Jill had assumed that once she was home, surrounded by everything that was familiar and comfortable, she'd be able to put their brief interlude behind her.

It hadn't happened.

Wednesday afternoon, Jill returned home from work, put water on for tea and began reading the evening paper. Normally she didn't glance at the financial section. She wasn't sure why she did now. Skimming the headlines, she idly folded back the page—and saw Jordan's name. It seemed to leap at her.

Jill's heart slowed, then vaulted into action as she read the article. He'd done it. The paper was reporting Jordan's latest coup. His company had reached an agreement with a land-management outfit in Hawaii, and construction on the shopping mall would begin sometime in the next three months.

He must be pleased. Although he hadn't said much, Jill knew Jordan had wanted this project to fly. A hundred questions bombarded her. Had he heard from Andrew Howard? Had the older man joined forces with Jordan, after all? Had he asked Jordan about her, and if so, what had Jordan told him? What could he possibly tell Mr. Howard about her now?

Jill had thought of writing Mr. Howard a note, but she didn't have his address. She didn't have Jordan's, either, but that didn't stop her.

Before she could determine the wisdom of her actions, she scribbled a few lines of congratulation, wrote Jordan's name on the envelope, along with the name of the building listed in the news article, and the next morning, mailed the card. She had no idea if it would even reach him.

Two days later when Jill returned home from work, she noticed a long luxury car parked in front of her apartment building. Other than giving it an inquisitive glance, she didn't pay any attention. She was shuffling through her purse searching for her keys when she heard someone approach from behind.

Tossing a look over her shoulder, she nearly dropped her purse. It was Jordan. He looked very much as he had the first time she'd seen him. Cynical and hard. Detached and unemotional. His smoky-gray eyes scanned her without revealing a hint of his thoughts. There was nothing to indicate he was glad to see her, or if he'd spared her a moment's thought since they'd parted. Nothing but cool indifference.

"Hello, Jill."

She was so flustered that the newspaper, which she'd tucked under her arm, fell to the floor. Stooping, she retrieved it, then clutched it against her chest as she straightened. "Jordan."

"I got your note."

"I—I wanted you to know how happy I was for you."

He was staring pointedly at her door.

"Um, would you like to come inside?" she asked, unlatching the door with fumbling fingers. "I'll make some tea if you like. Or coffee..." She hadn't expected this, nor was she emotionally prepared for seeing him. She hadn't anticipated him to do anything but read the card and then drop it into his wastebasket.

"Tea sounds fine."

"I'll just be a minute," she said as she hurried into the kitchen. Her heart was rampaging, pounding against her ribs. "Make yourself at home," she called out, holding the tea kettle under the faucet.

"You have a nice place," he said, standing in the doorway between the kitchen and the living room.

"Thank you. I've lived here for three years now." She didn't know why she'd told him that. It didn't matter to him how long she'd lived there.

"Why'd you send me the card?" he asked while she was setting out cups and saucers. She didn't feel comfortable using the mugs she did for everyday; she had a couple of lovely china cups her mother had given her and she'd decided on those instead. She paused at his question, frowning slightly. "To congratulate you."

"The real reason."

"That was the real reason. This shopping mall was important to you and I was happy to read that everything had finally come together. I knew you worked hard to make it happen. That was the only reason I wrote the note." Her cheeks warmed at his implication. He seemed to believe something she hadn't intended—or had she?

"Andrew Howard decided to invest in the project at the last minute. It was his support that made the difference."

Jill nodded. "I was hoping he would."

"I have you to thank for that."

Nothing in his expression indicated he was grateful for any assistance she might unwittingly have given him. His features remained cold and hard. The man who'd spent that day on the beach with her wasn't the harsh, unrelenting businessman who stood before her now.

"If I played any part in Mr. Howard's decision, I'm sure it was small."

"He seemed quite taken with you."

"I was quite taken with him, too."

A flicker of emotion passed through Jordan's eyes, one so fleeting, so transitory, she was sure she'd imagined it.

"I'd like to thank you, if you'd let me," he said.

She was dropping tea bags into her best ceramic teapot. "Thank me? You already have."

"I was thinking more along the lines of dinner."

Jill's first thought was that she didn't have anything appropriate to wear. Not to an elegant restaurant, and of course she couldn't imagine Jordan dining anywhere else. He wasn't exactly the kind of man who ate in a burger joint.

"Unless you already have plans . . ."

He was offering her an escape, and his eyes seemed to challenge her to take it.

"No," she said, almost gasping. Jill wasn't sure why she accepted so readily, why she didn't even consider declining. "I don't have anything planned for tonight."

"Is there a particular place you'd like to go?"

She shook her head. "You choose."

Jill felt a surge of excitement. She felt almost light-headed with happiness and anticipation. Trying to keep her voice steady, she added, "I'll need to change clothes, but that shouldn't take long."

He looked at her skirt and blouse as if seeing them for the first time. "You look fine just the way you are," he said, dismissing her concern.

The kettle whistled and Jill quickly removed it from the burner, pouring the scalding water into the teapot. "This should steep for a few minutes." She backed out of the kitchen, irrationally fearing that he'd disappear if she let him out of her sight.

She chose the same outfit she'd worn on the trip home—the Hawaiian print shirt with the hot pink flowers. The slacks weren't particularly dressy so she stepped into high heels. She put on the shell lei she'd purchased the first day she'd gone touring. Then she freshened her makeup and brushed her hair.

Jordan had poured the tea and was adding sugar to his cup when she entered the kitchen. His gaze didn't waver or change in any way, yet she could tell he liked her choice.

The phone rang. Jill darted a look at it, willing it to stop. She didn't know who would be phoning her now, but guessed it was probably Ralph. The man seemed to have an incredibly bad sense of timing.

"Hello," she said, hoping her voice didn't convey her lack of welcome.

"Jill, it's Shelly. How are you? I haven't heard a word from you since you got home. Are you all right? I've been worried. You generally phone once or twice a week. It's not like you to—"

"I'm fine."

"You're sure?"

"Positive." Talk about timing, Jill mused. Shelly's was worse than Ralph's!

"You sound preoccupied. Am I catching you at a bad time? Is Ralph there? Maybe he'll take the hint and go home. Honestly, Jill, I don't know why you continue to see that guy. I mean, he's nice, but he's about as romantic as mold."

"Uh, I have company."

"Company," Shelly echoed. "Who? No, let me guess. Jordan Wilcox!"

"Bingo."

"Talk to you later. Bye." The drone of the disconnected line sounded in her ear so fast that Jill was left holding the receiver for several seconds before she realized her friend had hung up.

No sooner had Jill replaced it when the phone rang again. She cast an apologetic glance toward Jordan and snatched up the receiver. "Hello."

"This is Shelly again. I want it understood that you're to give me a full report later."

"Shelly!"

"And don't you dare try to return that wedding dress. He's the one, Jill. Quit fighting it. I'll let you go now, but just remember, I want details, so be prepared." She hung up as quickly as she had the first time.

"That was my best friend."

"Shelly?"

Jill couldn't remember mentioning her to Jordan, but obviously she had. "She's married to Mark Brady." She waited, wondering if Jordan would recognize the name.

"Mark Brady." He tested it, as though saying it aloud would jar his memory. "Is Mark a tax consultant? I seem to remember hearing something about him not long ago. Isn't he the head of his own firm?"

"That's Mark." The story of how Shelly and Mark met nearly slipped out, but Jill stopped herself in the nick of time. Jordan knew about the wedding dress— though not its significance—because Jill had inadvertently let it slip that first night.

"And Mark's married to your best friend?"

"That's right." She took a sip of her tea. "When I mentioned I'd met you, Mark knew who you were right away."

"So you mentioned me." He seemed pleasantly surprised.

He could have no idea how much he'd been in her thoughts the past couple of weeks. She'd tried, heaven knew she'd tried, to push every memory of him from her mind. But it hadn't worked. She couldn't quite explain it, but somehow nothing was the same anymore.

"You're ready?" he asked after a moment.

Jill nodded and carried their empty cups to the sink. Then Jordan led her to his car, opening the door and ushering her inside. When he joined her, he reached for his ever-present phone, punched out one number, then asked that his calls be held.

"You don't need to do that on my account," she told him.

"I'm not," he said, his smile tight, almost a grimace. "I'm doing it for me." With that he started the engine.

Jill hadn't a clue where they were going. He took the freeway and headed north, exiting into the downtown area of Seattle. There were any number of four-star restaurants within a five-block area. Jill was curious, but she didn't ask. She'd know soon enough.

When Jordan pulled into the underground garage of a luxury skyscraper, Jill was momentarily surprised. But then several of the office complexes housed world-class restaurants.

"I didn't know there was a restaurant here," she said conversationally.

"There isn't."

"Oh."

"I live in the penthouse."

"Oh."

"Unless you object?"

"No...no, that's fine."

"I phoned earlier and asked the cook to prepare dinner for two."

"You have a cook?" Oddly, that fact amazed her, though she supposed it shouldn't have, considering his wealth.

He smiled, his first genuine smile since he'd shown up at her door. "You're easily impressed."

He made it sound as though everyone employed a cook, the way most people had a newspaper-delivery boy.

They rode a private elevator thirty floors up to the penthouse suite. The first thing that greeted Jill as the doors glided open was a breathtaking view of Puget Sound.

"This is beautiful," she whispered, stepping out. She followed him through his living room, past a white leather sectional sofa and a glass-and-chrome coffee table that held a small sculpture. She wasn't too knowledgeable when it came to works of art, but this looked like a collector's item.

"That's a Doug Graham piece," Jordan said matter-of-factly.

Jill nodded, hoping he wouldn't guess how ignorant she was.

"White wine?"

"Please." Jill couldn't take her eyes off the view. The waterways of Puget Sound were dotted with white-and-green ferries. The islands—Bainbridge, Whidbey and Vashon—were jewellike against the backdrop of the Olympic mountains.

"Nothing like Hawaii, is it?" Jordan asked as he handed her a long-stemmed wineglass.

"No, but just as beautiful in its own way."

"I'm headed back to Oahu next week."

"So soon?" Jill was envious.

"It's another short trip. Two or three days at most."

"Perhaps you'll get a chance to go snorkeling again."

Jordan shook his head. "I won't have time for any underwater adventures this trip," he told her.

Jill perched on the edge of the sofa, staring down at her wine. "I don't think I'll ever be able to separate you from my time in Oahu," she said softly. "The rest of my week seemed so... empty."

"I know what you mean."

Her heartbeat quickened as his gaze strayed to her mouth. He sat beside her and removed the wine goblet from her unresisting hand. Next his fingers curved around her neck, ever so lightly, brushing aside her hair. His eyes held hers as if he expected resistance. Then slowly, giving her ample opportunity to pull away if she wished, he lowered his mouth to hers.

Jill moaned in anticipation, instinctively moving closer. Common sense shouted in alarm, but she refused to listen. Just once she wanted to know what it was like to be kissed with real passion—to be cherished by a man. Just once she wanted to know what it meant to be adored. Her heart filled with a delirious joy. Her hands slid up his chest to his shoulders, as she clung to him. He kissed her again, small, nibbling kisses, as though he were afraid of frightening her with the strength of his need. But he must have sensed her receptiveness, because he deepened the kiss.

Suddenly it came to her. The same thing that had happened to Shelly was now happening to her. The phenomenon Aunt Milly had experienced fifty years earlier was coming to pass a third time.

The wedding dress.

Abruptly, she broke off the kiss. Panting, holding both hands over her heart, she sprang to her feet. Her eyes were wide and incredulous as she gazed down at a surprised Jordan.

"It's you!" she cried. "It really is you."

CHAPTER SIX

"WHAT DO YOU MEAN, it's me?" Jordan demanded. When she didn't answer, he asked, "What's wrong, Jill?"

"Everything," she cried, shaking her head.

"I hurt you?"

"No," she whispered, "no." She sobbed quietly as she wrung her hands. "I don't know what to do."

"Why do you have to do anything?"

"Because...oh, you wouldn't understand." Worse, she couldn't tell him. Every time he looked at her, she became more and more convinced that Shelly had been right. Jordan Wilcox was her future.

But she *couldn't* fall in love with him, because she knew what would happen to her if she did—she'd become like her mother, lonely, bitter and unhappy. If she was going to marry, she wanted a man who was safe and sensible. A man like...Ralph. Yet the thought of spending the rest of her life with Ralph produced an even deeper sense of discontent.

"I'm not an unreasonable man," Jordan said. Then he added, "Well, generally I'm not. If there's a problem you can tell me."

"It's not supposed to be a problem. According to Shelly and her Aunt Milly, it's a blessing. I know I'm talking in riddles, but . . . there's no way you'd understand!"

"Try me."

"I can't. I'm sorry, I just can't."

"But it has something to do with my kissing you?"

She stared at him blankly. "No. Yes."

"You seem rather uncertain about this. Perhaps we should try it again and see what happens."

"That isn't necessary." But even as she spoke, Jordan was reaching for her, pulling her down onto his lap. Jill willingly surrendered to his embrace, greeting his kiss with a muffled groan of welcome, a sigh of defeat. His arms held her close, and not for the first time, Jill was stunned by the effect he had on her. It left her feeling both unnerved and overwhelmed.

His lips, gentle and caressing, moved over her face. Jill felt as though she'd been swept into a whirlpool, and if she didn't do something to save herself it would soon be too late.

"Better?" he asked a moment later in a remarkably steady voice.

Unable to answer, Jill closed her eyes, then nodded. Better, yes. And worse. Every time he touched her, it confirmed what she feared most.

"I thought so." He seemed reassured, but that did little to comfort Jill. For weeks she'd played a silly game of denial. They'd met, and from that moment forth, nothing had been the same.

She didn't, couldn't, believe in the power of the wedding dress; she scoffed at the implausibility of its legend. Yet even Mr. Howard, who knew nothing about Aunt Milly and the old story, had felt compelled to explain Jordan's past to her, had seen Jill as his future.

She'd spent only three days with Jordan, but she knew more about him than she knew about Ralph, whom she'd been dating for months. Their day on the beach and the dinner with Andrew Howard had given her an insight into Jordan's personality. Since then Jill had found it more difficult to accept what she saw on the surface—the detached, cynical male. The man who wore his I-don't-give-a-damn attitude like an elaborate mask.

Perhaps she understood him because he was so much like her father. Adam Morrison had lived for the excitement, the risks, of the big deal. He poured his life's blood into each business transaction because he'd never really accepted the importance of family, emotion, human values.

Jordan wouldn't, either.

Dinner was a strained affair, although Jordan made several efforts to lighten the mood. As he drove her home, Jill sensed he wanted to say something more. Whatever it was, he left unsaid.

"Have a safe trip," she told him when he escorted her to her door. Her heart was pounding, not with excitement, but with trepidation, wondering if he planned to kiss her again. Fearing he did, praying he would.

"I'll call you when I get back," he told her. And that was all.

"THERE'S A SPECIAL fondness in my heart for this place," Shelly said as she slipped into a chair opposite Jill. They were meeting for lunch at Patrick's, a restaurant in the mall where Jill's branch of PayRite was located. Typically, she was ten minutes late. Marriage to Mark, who was habitually prompt, hadn't altered Shelly's tardiness. Jill often wondered how they managed to keep their love so strong when they were so different.

Patrick's had played a minor role in Shelly's romance with Mark. Jill recalled the Saturday she'd met her friend there for lunch, and how amused she'd been at Shelly's crazy story of receiving the infamous wedding dress.

Funny, that was exactly the way Jill felt now—frantic, frightened, confused. And strangely excited . . .

"So tell me everything," Shelly said breathlessly.

"Jordan stopped by. We had dinner. He left town this morning on a business trip," she explained dispassionately. "There isn't much to tell."

Shelly's hand closed around her water glass, her eyes connecting with Jill's. "Do you remember when I first met Mark?"

"I'm not likely to forget," Jill said, smiling despite her present mood.

"Any time you or my mother or anyone else asked me about Mark, I always said there wasn't anything to tell. Remember?"

"Yes." Jill remembered how Shelly's face would close, her voice grow abrupt, whenever anyone mentioned Mark's name.

"When I told you nothing was happening, I was stretching the truth a bit," Shelly continued. "A whole lot was going on, but nothing I felt I could share. Even with you." She raised her eyebrows. "You, my friend, are wearing the same look I did. A great deal has taken place between you and Jordan. So much that you're frightened out of your wits. Trust me, I know."

"He kissed me again," Jill admitted.

"It was better than before?"

"Worse!"

Shelly apparently found Jill's answer amusing. She tried to hide her smile behind the menu, then lowered it to say, "Don't count on your feelings becoming any less complicated. They won't."

"He's going to be away for a few days. Thank goodness, because it gives me time to think."

"Oh, Jill," Shelly said with a sympathetic sigh, "I wish there was something I could say to help you. Why are you fighting this so hard?" She grinned sheepishly. "I fought it, too. Be smart, just accept it. Love isn't really all that terrifying once you let go of your doubts."

"Instead of talking about Jordan, why don't we order lunch?" Jill suggested a little curtly. "I'm starved."

"Me, too."

The waitress arrived at their table a moment later, and Jill ordered the split-pea soup and a turkey sandwich.

"Just a minute," Shelly interrupted, motioning toward the waitress. She turned to Jill. "You don't even *like* split-pea soup. You never order it." She gave Jill an odd look, then turned back to the waitress. "She'll have the clam chowder."

"Shelly!"

The waitress wrote down the order quickly, as though she feared an argument was about to erupt.

"You're more upset than I realized," Shelly said when they were alone. "Ordering split-pea soup—I can't believe it."

"It's soup, Shelly, not nuclear waste." Her friend definitely had a tendency to overreact. It drove Jill crazy, but it was the very thing that made Shelly so endearing.

"I'm going to call Jordan Wilcox myself," Shelly announced suddenly.

"You're going to *what?*" It was all Jill could do to remain in her seat.

"You heard me."

"Shelly, no! I absolutely forbid you to discuss me with Jordan. How would you have felt if I'd called Mark?"

Shelly's frown deepened. "I'd have been furious."

"I will be, too, if you say so much as one word to Jordan about me."

Shelly paused, her eyes wide with concern. "But I'm afraid you're going to mess this up."

Nothing to fear there—Jill already had. She reached for a package of rye crisps from the bread basket, as Shelly frowned. It wasn't until then that she realized she wasn't any fonder of rye crisps than she was of split-pea soup.

"Promise me you'll stay out of it," Jill pleaded. "Please," she added for extra measure.

"All right," Shelly muttered. "Just don't do anything stupid."

"THIS IS A PLEASANT surprise," Jill's mother said as she opened the front door. Elaine Morrison was in her mid-fifties, slim and attractive.

"I thought I'd bring over your gift from Hawaii," Jill said, following her mother into the kitchen where Elaine automatically poured them tall glasses of iced tea. Jill set the box of chocolate-covered macadamia nuts on the counter.

"I'm glad your vacation went so well."

Jill pulled out a bar stool and sat at the counter, trying to look relaxed when she was anything but. "I met someone while I was in Hawaii."

Her mother paused, then smiled. "I thought you might have."

"What makes you say that?"

"Oh, there's a certain look about you. Now tell me how you met, what he's like, where he's from and what he does for a living."

Jill couldn't help laughing at the rapid-fire questions.

Elaine added slices of lemon to their tea and started across the kitchen, a new excitement in her step. Finally, after fifteen years, her mother was beginning to overcome the bitterness, the sense of loss, her husband's obsession with business had created. She was finally coming to terms with her grief over his neglect, and his death.

Jill was relieved and delighted by the signs of her mother's recovery, but she had to say, "Frankly, Mom, I don't think you'll like him."

Her mother looked surprised. "Whyever not?"

Jill didn't hesitate, didn't pause. "Because he reminds me of Daddy."

Her mother's eyes widened with shock, and tears sprang to her eyes. "Jill, no. For the love of heaven, no."

"I'VE BEEN GIVING some thought to your suggestion," Jill said to Ralph a few hours later. Her nerves were in turmoil. The clam chowder sat like a dead weight in the pit of her stomach, and her mother's dire warnings had badly shaken her.

Ralph wasn't tall and strikingly handsome like Jordan, but he was a comfortable sort of man. He made a person feel at ease. In fact, his laid-back manner was a blessed relief after the high-stress, high-energy hours she'd spent with Jordan, few though they were.

Jordan Wilcox could pull together a deal for an apartment complex before Ralph stepped out of the shower in the morning. Ralph's idea of an exhilarating evening was doing the newspaper crossword puzzle.

Everything about Jordan was complex. Everything about Ralph was uncomplicated; he was a straightforward, honest man who'd be a good husband and a loving father.

"Are you saying what I think you're saying?" Ralph prompted when she didn't immediately continue.

Jill cupped her water glass. "You said something not long ago about the two of us giving serious consideration to making our relationship permanent and...and I wanted you to know I was...I was giving some thought to that myself lately."

Ralph didn't reveal any emotion. He put down his hamburger, looked her way and asked casually, "Why now?"

"Uh...I'm going to be twenty-nine soon." She was outwardly calm, but her heart was pounding like a sledgehammer.

She was the biggest coward who ever lived. But what else could she do? Her mother had become nearly hysterical when Jill had told her about Jordan. Her own heart was filled with trepidation. On one hand there was Shelly, so confident Jordan was the man for Jill. On the other was her mother, adamant that Jill would be forever sorry if she got involved with a workaholic.

Jill was trapped somewhere in the middle, frightened and unsure.

Ralph relaxed against the red vinyl upholstery. The diner was his favorite place to eat, and he took her there every time they dined out. "So you think we should seriously consider marriage?"

It was the subject Jill had been leading up to all evening, yet when Ralph directly posed the question, she hesitated. If only Jordan hadn't kissed her. If only he hadn't held her in his arms. And if only she hadn't spoken to her mother.

"I missed you while you were away," Ralph said, his gaze holding hers.

Jill knew this was about as close to romance as she was likely to get from Ralph. Romance was his weakest suit, dependability and steadiness his strongest. Ralph would always be there by his wife's side. He'd make the kind of father who played catch in the backyard with his son. The kind of father who would bring his wife and daughter pretty pink corsages on Easter morning. He was a rock, a fortress of permanence. If only she could fall in love with him....

Jordan might have a talent for making millions, but all the money in the world couldn't buy happiness.

"I missed you, too," Jill said softly. She'd thought of Ralph, had wondered about him. A few times, anyway. Hadn't she mailed him a postcard? Hadn't she brought him back a book on volcanoes?

"I'm glad to hear that," Ralph said, and then clearing his throat, added, "Jill Morrison, will you do me the honor of becoming my wife?"

The question was out now, ready for her to answer. A proposal was what she'd been hinting for all evening. Now that Ralph had asked, Jill wasn't sure what she felt. Relief? No, it wasn't even close to that. Pleasure? Yes—in a way. But not a throw-open-the-windows-and-shout kind of joy.

Joy. The word hit her like an unanticipated punch. Joy was what she'd experienced the first time Jordan had taken her in his arms. A free-flowing joy and the promise of so much more.

The promise she was rejecting out of fear. Ralph might not be the love of her life, but he'd care for her and devote his life to her. It was enough. She could live with enough.

"Jill?" he prompted.

She tried to smile, tried to look happy and excited. Ralph deserved that much. "Yes," she whispered, stretching her hand across the table for him to take. "Yes, I'll marry you."

"WHAT DO YOU MEAN you're engaged to marry Ralph?" Shelly demanded. Her voice had risen to such a high pitch that Jill held the telephone receiver away from her ear.

"He asked me tonight and I've accepted."

"You can't *do* that!" her friend shrieked.

Jill ignored her outrage. "Of course I can."

"What about Jordan?" Shelly asked next.

"I'd already decided not to see him again." Jill was able to keep her composure, although she found it difficult.

"If marrying Ralph is typical of your recent decisions, then I'd like to suggest you talk to a mental-health professional."

Jill laughed despite herself. Her decision had been based on maintaining her sanity, not destroying it.

"I don't know what's so funny. I just can't believe you'd do something like this! What about Aunt Milly's wedding dress? Doesn't that mean anything to you? Don't you care that Mark, Aunt Milly and I all felt the dress should go to you next? You can't ignore it. Something dreadful might happen."

"Don't be ridiculous."

"I'm not," Shelly insisted resolutely. "You're playing with fire here. You can't reject the man destiny has chosen for you without serious consequences." Shelly's voice was growing more solemn by the second.

"You don't know that Jordan's the man," Jill said with far more conviction than she was feeling. "We both know a wedding dress can't dictate who I'll marry. The choice is mine—and I've chosen Ralph."

"You're honestly choosing Ralph over Jordan?" The question had an incredulous quality.

"Yes."

There was a moment's silence.

"You're running scared," Shelly went on, "frightened half out of your wits because of everything you feel. I know, because I went through the same thing. Jill, please, think about this before you do something you'll regret the rest of your life."

"I have thought about it," she insisted. She'd thought of little else since her last encounter with Jordan. Since her talk with Shelly. Since her visit to her mother's. She'd carefully weighed her options. Marrying Ralph seemed the best course.

"You have no intention of changing your mind, do you?" Shelly cried. "Do you honestly expect me to stand by and do nothing while you ruin your life?"

"I'm not ruining my life. Don't be absurd." Her voice grew hard. "Naturally I'll return your Aunt Milly's wedding dress and—"

"No," Shelly groaned. "Here, talk to Mark before I say something I shouldn't."

"Jill?" Mark came on the line. "What's the problem?"

Jill didn't want to repeat everything. She was tired and it was late and all she wanted to do was go to bed. Escape for the next eight hours and then face the world again. Jill hadn't intended to tell Shelly and Mark her news quite so soon, but there had been a telephone message from them when she arrived home. She'd decided she might as well let Shelly know of her decision. Jill wasn't sure what she'd expected from her friends, but certainly not this.

"Just a minute," Mark said next. "Shelly's trying to tell me something."

Although Shelly had given the phone to her husband, Jill could hear her friend's frantic words as clearly as if she still held the receiver. Shelly was pleading with Mark to talk some sense into Jill, begging him to try because she hadn't been able to change Jill's mind.

"Mark," Jill called, but apparently he didn't hear her. "Mark," she tried again, louder this time.

"I'm sorry, Jill," he said politely, "but Shelly's upset, and I'm having a hard time figuring out just what the problem is. All I can make out is that you've decided not to see Jordan Wilcox again."

"I'm marrying Ralph Emery, and I don't think he'd take kindly to my dating Jordan."

Mark chuckled. "No, I don't suppose he would. Frankly, I believe the decision is yours, and yours alone. I know Jordan, I've talked to him a couple of times and I share your concerns. I can't picture him married."

"He's already married," Jill stated unemotionally, "to his job. A wife would only stand in the way."

"That's probably true. What about Ralph—have I met him?"

"I don't think so," Jill returned stiffly. "He's a very nice man. Honest and hardworking. Shelly seems to think he's dull, and perhaps he is in some ways, but he...cares for me. It isn't a great love match, but we're both aware of that."

"Shelly thinks I'm dull, too, but that didn't stop her from marrying me."

Mark was so calm, so reassuring. He was exactly what Jill needed. She was so grateful she felt close to tears. "I want to do the right thing," she said, sucking in a small breath. Her voice wavered and she bit her lower lip, blinking rapidly.

"It's difficult knowing what's right sometimes, isn't it?" Mark said quietly. "I remember how I felt the first time I met Shelly. Here was this completely bizarre woman announcing to everyone who'd listen that she refused to marry me. I hadn't even asked—didn't even know her name. Then we stumbled on each other a second time and a third, and finally I learned about Aunt Milly's wedding dress."

"What did you think when she told you?"

"That it was the most ridiculous thing I'd ever heard."

"I did, too. I still do." She wanted a husband, *but not Jordan.*

"I'm sure you'll make the right decision," Mark said confidently.

"I am, too. Thanks, Mark, I really appreciate talking to you." The more she grew to know her friend's husband, the more Jill realized how perfectly the two suited each other. Mark brought a wonderful balance into Shelly's life, and she'd infused his with her warmth and wit. If only she, Jill, could have met someone like Mark.

No sooner had she hung up the phone when there was a loud knock on her door. Since it was late, close to eleven, Jill was surprised.

Peering through the peephole in the door, she gasped and drew away. Jordan Wilcox.

"I thought you were in Hawaii," she said as she opened the door.

"I was." His eyes scanned her hungrily. "This morning I had the most incredible feeling something was wrong. I tried to phone, but there wasn't any answer."

"I . . . was out for most of the day."

He gripped her shoulders and then, before she could protest, dragged her into his arms.

"Jordan?" She'd never seen him like this, didn't understand why he seemed so disturbed.

"I just couldn't shake the feeling something was terribly wrong with you."

"I'm fine."

"I know," he said, inhaling deeply. "Thank God you're safe."

CHAPTER SEVEN

"OF COURSE I'M SAFE," Jill insisted, as surprised as she was bewildered. Jordan's arms were tight around her and he buried his head in the curve of her neck, his breathing hard.

"I've never experienced anything like this before," he said, loosening his hold. His hands caressed the length of her arms as he moved back one small step. He studied her, his gaze intimate and tender. "I hope nothing like this ever happens to me again." Taking her hand, he led her to the sofa.

"You're not making any sense."

"I know." He momentarily closed his eyes, then gave a deep sigh. Gripping her fingers with his own, he raised them to his lips and gently kissed the back of her hand.

"It was the most unbelievable thing," he continued, with a small shrug of his shoulders. "I awoke with this feeling of impending doom. At first I tried to ignore it, pretend it didn't exist. But as the day wore on I couldn't shake it. All I knew was that it had something to do with you.

"I thought if I talked to you I could assure myself nothing was wrong, that this feeling would go away. Only I wasn't able to get hold of you."

"I was out most of the day," she repeated unnecessarily.

Jordan rubbed a hand down his face. "When I tried to phone and couldn't get an answer, I panicked. I booked the next flight to Seattle."

"What about your business in Hawaii?"

"I canceled one meeting and left what I could with an assistant. Everything's taken care of." He sighed once more and sagged against the back of her sofa. "I could do with a cup of coffee."

"Of course." Jill immediately stood and hurried into her compact kitchen, starting the coffee and assembling cups and saucers in a matter of minutes. She was arranging everything on a tray when Jordan stepped up behind her.

He slid his arms around her waist and kissed the side of her neck. "I don't know what's happening between us."

"I...don't know that anything is."

Jordan chuckled softly, the sound a gentle caress against her skin. "I'm beginning to think you've cast a spell over me."

Jill froze. "Spell" and "magic" were words she'd rather not hear. A lump the size of Texas filled her throat. Even the smallest hint that the wedding dress was affecting him wouldn't change what she'd done. She'd made her decisions. The dress was packed away in the box Shelly had mailed her, ready to be returned.

"I've never experienced anything like this before," Jordan said again, sounding almost uncertain.

Jill should have been shocked. Jordan Wilcox had probably never felt confused or doubtful about anything in his adult life. She speculated that his emotions had been buried so deep, hidden by pride for so long, that he barely recognized them anymore.

"I think I'm falling in love with you."

Jill gasped and closed her eyes. She didn't want to hear this, didn't want to deal with a declaration of love. Not now. Not when she'd settled everything in her own mind. Not when she'd reconciled herself to never seeing him again.

"That's not true," Jordan countered evenly, twisting her around and into his arms. "I can't live without you. I've known that from the first moment we kissed."

"Oh, no..."

The sound of his amusement filled her small kitchen. "You said the same thing that night, too. Remember?" The smile faded as he gazed at her upturned face. His eyes, so gray and intense, seemed to sear her with a look of such power it was all Jill could do not to cry out and break off his embrace. She glanced away, chewing nervously on her lower lip, willing him to free her, willing him to leave before she changed her mind.

His hands cupped her face, his thumbs stroking her cheeks. "You feel it, too, don't you?" he whispered.

"You have from the very first. Neither one of us can deny it."

She meant to tell him then, to blurt out that she was engaged to Ralph, but she wasn't given the chance. Before she could utter a word, before she could even begin to explain, Jordan captured her mouth with his own.

His lips were hard and desperate as they claimed possession of hers, firing her senses to life. She moaned, not from pleasure, although that was keen, but from regret.

Ralph had kissed her that night, too. Jill had tried so hard to reassure herself their marriage would work. She'd put her heart and her soul into their good-night kiss and hadn't experienced even a fraction of what she did with Jordan.

It was so unfair, so wrong. She was marrying Ralph, her mind shouted. But her heart, her foolish, romantic heart, refused to listen.

Nothing Jordan could say was going to change her plans, she decided, forcing herself to think of Ralph and the commitment they'd made to each other only a few hours earlier.

If only Jordan would stop kissing her. *Oh, please stop,* she begged silently as frustration brought burning tears to her eyes. If only he'd leave, walk out of her life forever so she could start forgetting.

But she had to push him out of her arms before she could push him out of her life. Yet here she was clinging to him, her arms, her traitorous arms, curved around his neck. And she was holding on as though her life depended on it.

Jordan obviously felt none of her hesitation, none of her doubts. He went on numbing her senses with his kisses and soon, far too soon, Jill was returning them with equal fervor. Raw emotion overwhelmed her until she was so weak she slumped against him, needing his support to remain upright. Her breath came in shallow gasps as his lips trembled against hers.

"Oh, Jill," he breathed, his voice a husky caress. "The things you do to me. I've frightened you, haven't I?"

"No." He had, but for none of the reasons he knew. She was terrified by the things he made her feel. Terrified by the rush of need and love that crowded her heart.

She buried her face in his shoulder, wanting to escape his arms even as she submerged herself in them.

"I never knew love could be like this," Jordan said hoarsely. "I've never been in love, never experienced it before you." He rested his jaw alongside her cheek in a gesture of tenderness that moved her deeply.

Jill swallowed against the tightness blocking her throat and blinked through a wall of tears. "Please..." She had to say something, had to let him know before he spoke again, before he convinced her to love him. She'd set her mind, her will, everything within her, to resist him and found she couldn't.

"I realize we haven't known each other long," Jordan was saying. "Yet it seems as if you've always been a part of my life, always will be."

"No..."

"Yes," he countered softly, his lips grazing the side of her face. "I want to marry you, Jill. Soon. The sooner the better. I need you in my life. I need you to teach me so many things. Loving me isn't going to be easy, but—"

"No!" Abruptly she broke away from him, although it demanded every ounce of energy she possessed. "Please, no." She buried her face in her hands and began to sob.

"Jill, what is it?" He tried to comfort her, tried to bring her back into his embrace, but she wouldn't let him.

"I can't marry you." The words, born of frustration and anger, were meant to be shouted, but by the time they passed her lips they were barely audible.

"Can't marry me?" Jordan repeated as though he was sure he'd misunderstood. "Why not?"

"Because..." Saying it became nearly an impossible task, but she forced herself. "Because...I'm already engaged."

She saw and felt his shock. His eyes narrowed with disbelief and pain as the color drained from his face, leaving him pale beneath his tan.

"You're making it up."

"No, it's true." She held herself stiff, braced for the backlash her words were sure to bring.

"When?" he demanded.

She heaved in a breath and squared her shoulders. "Tonight."

A shudder went through him as his eyes, dark and haunting, raked her face. Jill's throat muscles constricted at his tortured look, and she couldn't speak, couldn't explain.

It took Jordan a moment to compose himself. But he did so with amazing dexterity. All emotion fled from his face. For a breathless moment he just stared at her.

"I'm sure," he said finally, without any outward hint of regret, "whoever it is will make you a far better husband than I would have."

"His name is Ralph."

Jordan grimaced, but quickly rearranged his features into a cool mask. "I wish you and...Ralph every happiness."

With that, he turned and walked out of her life.

EARLY THE NEXT MORNING, after an almost sleepless night, Jill carted the infamous wedding dress to her car and drove directly to Shelly and Mark's. The curtains were open so she assumed they were up and about. Even if they weren't, she didn't care.

Keeping the wedding dress a moment longer was intolerable. The thing was an albatross around her neck. The sooner she was rid of it, the sooner her life would return to normal.

Jill locked her car and carried the box to the Bradys' front door. Her steps were crisp and impatient. If Shelly wasn't home, Jill swore she'd leave the wedding gown on the front steps rather than take it back to her apartment.

A few minutes passed before the door opened. Shelly stood on the other side, dressed in a long robe, her hair in disarray and her hand covering her mouth to hide a huge, shoulder-raising yawn.

"I got you out of bed?" That much was obvious, but Jill was in no state for intelligent conversation.

"I was awake," Shelly said, yawning again. "Mark had to go into the office early this morning, but I couldn't make myself get up." She gestured Jill inside. "Come on in. I'm sure Mark made a pot of coffee. He knows I need a cup first thing in the morning."

Jill set the box down on the sofa and followed Shelly into the kitchen. Clearly her friend wasn't fully awake yet, so Jill walked over to the cupboards and collected two mugs, filling each with coffee, then bringing them to the table where Shelly was sitting.

"Oh, thanks," she mumbled. "I'm impossible until I've had my first cup."

"I seem to remember that from our college days."

"Right," Shelly said, managing a half smile. "You know all my faults. Can you believe Mark loves me in spite of the fact that I can't cook, can't tolerate mornings and am impossibly disorganized?"

Having seen the love in Mark's eyes when he looked at his wife, Jill could well believe it. "Yes."

"I'm glad you're here," Shelly said, resting her head on her arm, which was stretched across the kitchen table.

"You are?" It was apparent that Shelly hadn't guessed the reason for this unexpected visit, hadn't realized Jill intended to return the wedding dress.

Half-asleep as she was, she obviously hadn't noticed the box.

"Yes, I'm *delighted* you're here," Shelly said as her eyes drifted shut. "Mark and I had a long talk about you and Ralph. He seems to think I'm overreacting to this engagement thing. But you aren't going to marry Ralph—you know it and I know it. This engagement is a farce, even if you don't recognize that yet. I know you, Jill. In some ways I know you as well as I do myself. Getting Ralph to propose is the only way you can deal with what's happening between you and Jordan. But you'd never go through with it. You're too honest. You won't let yourself cheat Ralph—because if you marry him, that's exactly what you'll be doing."

"He knows I don't love him."

"I'm sure he does, but I'm also sure he believes that in time you'll feel differently. What he doesn't understand is that you're already in love with someone else."

A few hours earlier, Jill would have adamantly denied loving Jordan, but she couldn't any longer. Her heart burned with the intensity of her feelings. Still, it didn't change anything, didn't alter the path she'd chosen.

"Ralph doesn't know about Jordan, does he?"

"No," Jill said reluctantly. If she was forced to, she'd tell Ralph about him. Difficult as it was to admit, Shelly was right. Jill would never be able to marry Ralph unless she was completely honest with him.

Shelly straightened and took her first sip of coffee. It seemed to revive her somewhat. "I should apologize for what I said last night. I didn't mean to offend you."

"You didn't," Jill was quick to assure her.

"You frightened me."

"Why?"

"I was afraid for you, afraid you were going to ruin your life. I don't think I could stand idly by and allow you to do it."

"I fully intend to marry Ralph." Jill didn't know for whose benefit she was saying this—Shelly's or her own. The doubts were back, but she did her best to ignore them.

"I'm sure you do intend to marry Ralph...now," Shelly continued, "but when the time comes, I have every confidence it won't happen. So does Mark."

"That isn't what he said when we talked." Mark had been the cool voice of reason in their impassioned discussion the night before. He'd reassured her and comforted her, and for that Jill would always be grateful.

"What he said," Shelly explained between giant yawns, "was that he was sure you'd make the right decision. And he is. I was, too, after he calmed me down."

"I've made my choice. There's no turning back now."

"You'll change your mind."

"Perhaps. I don't know. All I know right now is that I agreed to marry Ralph." No matter how hard she tried, she couldn't keep the breathless catch from her voice.

Shelly heard it, and her eyes slowly opened. "What happened?" Her gaze sharply assessed Jill, who tried not to say or do anything that would give her away.

"Tell me," she said when Jill hesitated. "You know I'll get it out of you one way or another."

Jill sighed. Hiding the truth would do little good. "Jordan stopped in late last night."

"I thought you said he was in Hawaii."

"He was."

"Then what was he doing at your place?" The question was sharp, insistent.

"He said he felt there was something wrong—and he flew home."

"There *is* something wrong!" Shelly cried. "You're engaged to the wrong man."

Wrong. Wrong. Wrong. Unexpectedly, Jill felt defeated. She'd hardly slept the night before, and the tears she'd managed to hold at bay refused to be held back any longer. They brimmed in her eyes, spilling onto her cheeks, cool against her flushed skin.

"I'm not engaged to the wrong man," she said once she was able to speak coherently. "I happen to love the wrong one."

"If you're in love with Jordan," Shelly said, "and I believe you are, then why in heaven's name would you even consider marrying Ralph?"

It was too difficult to explain, too difficult to put into words. Rather than make the effort, she merely shook her head and stood, almost toppling her chair in her eagerness to escape.

"Jill." Shelly stood, too.

"I have to go now..."

"Jill, what's wrong? My goodness, I've never seen you like this. Tell me."

Jill shook her head again and hurried into the living room. "I brought back the wedding dress. Thank your Aunt Milly for me, but I can't...wear it."

"You brought back the dress?" Shelly sounded as though she was about to break into tears herself. "Oh, Jill, I wish you hadn't."

Jill didn't stick around to argue. She rushed out the front door and to her car. Her destination wasn't clear until she reached Ralph's apartment. She hadn't planned to go there and wasn't sure what had directed her there. For several minutes she sat outside, collecting her thoughts, gathering her courage.

When she'd composed herself, blown her nose and dried her eyes, she walked to his front door and rang the doorbell. Ralph answered, looking pleased to see her.

"Good morning. You're out and about early. I was just about ready to leave for work."

She forced a smile. "Have you got a minute?"

"Sure. Come in." He paused and seemed to remember that they were now an engaged couple. He leaned forward and lightly brushed his lips across her cheek.

"I should have phoned first."

"No. I was just thinking that this afternoon might be a good time for us to look at engagement rings."

Jill guiltily dropped her gaze and her voice trembled. "That's very sweet." She could barely say the words she had to say. "I should explain . . . the reason I'm here—"

Ralph motioned her toward a chair. "Please, sit down."

Jill was grateful because she wasn't sure how much longer her legs would support her. Everything seemed so much more difficult in the light of day. She'd been so confident before, so sure she and Ralph could make a life together. Now she felt as though she were walking around in a heavy fog. Nothing was clear, and confusion greeted her at every turn.

She took a deep breath. "There's something I need to explain."

"Sure." Ralph sat comfortably across from her.

She was so close to the edge of the chair she was in danger of slipping off. "It's only fair you should know." She hesitated, thinking he might say something, but when he didn't, she continued, "I met a man in Hawaii."

He nodded gravely. "I thought you must have."

His intuition surprised her. "His name . . . Oh, it doesn't matter what his name is. We went out a couple of times."

"Are you in love with him?" Ralph asked outright.

"Yes," Jill whispered slowly, regretfully. It hurt to admit, and for a moment she dared not look at Ralph.

"It doesn't seem like a lot of time to be falling in love with a man. You were only gone a week."

Jill didn't tell him Jordan was in Hawaii only three days. Nor did she mention the two brief times she'd seen him since. She couldn't see that it would do any good to analyze the relationship. It was over. She'd made certain of that when she told him she was marrying Ralph. She'd never hear from Jordan again.

"Love happens like that sometimes," was the only answer Jill had.

"If you're so in love with this other guy, then why did you agree to marry me?"

"Because I'm frightened and, oh, Ralph, I'm so sorry. I should never have involved you in this. You're a wonderful man and I care for you, I honestly do. You've been a good friend and I've enjoyed our times together, but I realized this morning that I can't marry you."

For a moment he said nothing, then he reached for her hand and held it gently between his own. "You don't need to feel so guilty about it."

"But I do." She was practically drowning in guilt.

"Don't. It took me about two minutes to realize something was troubling you last night. You surprised me completely when you started talking about getting married."

"I surprised you?"

"To be honest, I assumed you were about to tell me you'd met someone else and wouldn't be seeing me any longer. I've known for a long time that you don't love me."

"But I believed that would've changed," Jill said almost desperately.

"That's what I figured, too."

"You're steady and dependable, and I need that in my life," she said, although the rationale sounded poor even to her own ears. True, if she married Ralph she wouldn't have the love match she'd always dreamed about, but she'd told herself that love was highly overrated. She'd decided she could live without love, live without passion—until Jordan showed up on her doorstep. And that morning, Shelly had told her what she already knew. She couldn't marry Ralph.

"You're here because you want to call off the engagement, aren't you?" Ralph asked.

Miserably, Jill nodded. "I didn't mean to hurt you. That's the last thing I want."

"You haven't," he said pragmatically. "I figured you'd call things off sooner or later."

"You did?"

He grinned sheepishly. "You going to marry this other man?"

Jill shrugged. "I don't know."

"If you do..."

"Yes?" Jill reluctantly raised her eyes to his.

"If you do, would you consider subletting your apartment to me? Your place is at least twice as big as mine, and your rent's cheaper."

Jill started to laugh. She didn't know where she found the energy, but the humor bubbled up inside her like fizz in a flute of champagne. Leave it to Ralph, ever practical, ever sensible, to brush off a broken engagement and ask about subletting her apartment.

THE WEEK THAT FOLLOWED was one of the worst of Jill's life. She awoke every morning feeling as though she hadn't slept. She was depressed and lonely. Several times she found herself close to tears for no apparent reason. She'd be reading a prescription and the words would blur and misery would grip her heart with such intensity she'd be forced to swallow a sob.

"Jill," her supervisor called early Friday afternoon, walking into the back room where she was taking her lunch break. "There's someone out front who wants to talk to you."

It was unusual for anyone to visit her at work. She immediately feared it was Jordan, but she quickly dismissed that concern. She knew him too well. She was out of his life. The instant she'd told him she was engaged to Ralph, he'd cut her out, surgically removed all emotion for her. It was as if she no longer existed for him.

But as she'd been so often lately, Jill was wrong. Jordan stood there waiting for her. His gaze was as hard as flint. Something flickered briefly in the smoky-gray depths, but whatever emotion he felt at seeing her was too fleeting for Jill to identify.

She'd had far less practice at hiding her own feelings, and right now, they were wreaking havoc with her pulse. With great effort she managed to remain outwardly composed. "You wanted to speak to me?"

A nerve twitched in his jaw. "You might be more comfortable if we spoke elsewhere," he said stiffly.

Jill glanced at her watch. She had only fifteen minutes of her lunch break left. Time enough, she was sure, for whatever Jordan intended. "All right."

Wordlessly, he walked out of the drugstore, obviously expecting her to follow, which she did. He paused in front of his car, then turned to face her. A cool, disinterested smile slanted his mouth.

"Yes?" she said after an awkward moment. She folded her arms defensively around her middle. If only he didn't look compelling, so wonderfully male.

"I need you to explain something."

She nodded. "I'll try."

"Your friend Shelly Brady was in to see me this morning."

Jill groaned inwardly. She hadn't talked to Shelly since the morning she'd dropped off the wedding dress. Her friend had phoned several times and left messages, but Jill hadn't either the energy or the patience to return the calls.

"How she managed to get past my secretary and my two assistants is beyond me."

It was a nightmare come true. "What did she say?" As if Jill needed to know.

"She rambled on about how you were making the worst mistake of your life and how I'd be an even bigger fool if I let you. But, you know, if you prefer to marry Roger, then that's your prerogative."

"His name is Ralph," she corrected.

"It doesn't make much difference to me."

"I didn't think it would," she said, keeping her gaze lowered to the black asphalt of the parking lot.

"Then she started telling me this ridiculous story about a legend behind a certain wedding dress."

Jill's eyes closed in frustration. "It's a bunch of foolishness."

"It certainly didn't make too much sense, especially the part about the dress fitting her and her marrying Mark. But she insisted that I realize the dress also fits you."

"Don't take Shelly seriously. She seems to put a lot of credence in that dress. Personally, I think the whole thing's a fluke. You don't need to worry about it."

"*Then* she told me this ridiculous tale about a vision she had of you in Hawaii and how happy you looked. It didn't make any more sense than the rest."

"I don't think you need to worry. Shelly means well, but she doesn't understand. The wedding dress is beautiful, but it isn't meant for me. The whole thing is ridiculous—you said so yourself, and I agree with you."

"That's what I thought—at first. A magic wedding dress makes about as much sense as a talking rabbit. I don't believe in such nonsense."

"Then why are you here?"

"Because I remembered something. You had a wedding dress with you in Hawaii. When I asked you about it, you said a friend had mailed it to you. Then, this morning, Shelly arrived and started explaining why she'd sent you the dress. She told me the story about her Aunt Milly and how she'd met her husband. She also explained how Milly had mailed the dress to her and she'd fallen into Mark Brady's arms."

"Did she leave anything out?" Jill asked sarcastically.

He ignored her question. "In the end I phoned Mark and asked him about it. I don't know Brady well, but I figured he'd be able to explain matters a little more rationally."

"Shelly does tend to get a bit dramatic."

"She's your friend."

"Yes, I know. It's just that I wish she hadn't said anything to you."

"I imagine you do," he remarked dryly.

"What did Mark say?"

"We talked for several minutes. By this time Shelly was weeping and nearly hysterical, convinced she was saving us both from a fate worse than death. Mark was kind enough to inject a bit of sanity into the discussion. What it boiled down to is this."

"What?" Jill wasn't purposely being obtuse.

"Me confronting you. I'm here to ask you about Aunt Milly's wedding dress."

He could ask her what he wanted, but she didn't have any answers.

"Jill?"

She heaved a sigh. "I returned the dress to Shelly."

"She explained that, too. Said you'd brought it back the morning after my visit."

"It wasn't meant for me."

"Not true, according to Shelly and Mark." He remained standing where he was, hard and unyielding, unwilling to divulge his own feelings.

"So you're going to go ahead and marry Roger."

"Ralph."

"Whoever," Jordan snapped.

"No!" she shouted, furious with him, furious with Shelly and Mark, too.

A moment of shocked silence followed her announcement. Several feet separated Jill from Jordan, and although neither of them moved, they suddenly seemed much closer.

"I know," he said after a moment.

"How could you possibly know?" Jill hadn't told anyone yet. Not Shelly and certainly not Jordan.

"Because you're marrying me."

CHAPTER EIGHT

ALL JILL'S DEFENSES came tumbling down. She'd known they would from the moment Jordan had first kissed her. Known from the moment she'd walked out of the lunchroom and confronted him. Known in the very depths of her soul that he would eventually have his way. She hadn't the strength to fight him any longer.

He must have sensed her acquiescence because he moved toward her, pausing just short of taking her in his arms. "You will marry me, won't you?" The words were gentle yet insistent, brooking no argument.

Jill nodded. "I don't want...don't want to love you."

"I know." He reached for her then, drawing her into his embrace as though he were comforting a child.

It should have eased her mind that settling into his arms felt more natural than anything she'd done in the past week. A feeling of welcome. A feeling of rightness. And yet there was fear.

"You're going to break my heart," she whispered.

"Not if I can help it."

"Why do you want to marry me?" The answer evaded her. A man like Jordan could have his pick of women. He had wealth and prestige and a dozen other attributes that attracted far more sophisticated and far more beautiful women than Jill.

The air between them seemed to pulse for long moments before Jordan answered. "I've done some thinking about that myself. You're intelligent. Insightful. You feel things deeply and you're sensitive to the needs of others." He traced a finger along the line of her jaw, his touch light, feather-soft. "You're passionate about the people you love."

She should have been reassured that he seemed to know her so well after such a short acquaintance, but she wasn't. Because she knew that for a time she'd be a welcome distraction. Their marriage would be like a toy to him, then gradually as the newness wore off, she'd be put on a shelf to look pretty and brought down when it suited his purposes. His life, his love, his personality, would be consumed by the drive to succeed, just the way her father's had been. Everything else faded into the background, to eventually disappear. Love. Family. Commitment. All that was important to her would ultimately mean nothing to him.

"I want us to marry soon," Jordan whispered as his chin stroked the crown of her head.

"I—I was hoping for a long engagement."

Jordan's eyes were adamant. "I've waited too long already."

Jill didn't understand what he meant, but she didn't question him. She knew Jordan was an impatient man and always had been. When he wanted something, he went after it with relentless determination. Now he wanted her—and heaven help her, she wanted him.

"A bride should be happy," he said, tucking his hand under her chin and raising her face to his. "Why the tears?"

How could she possibly explain her fears? She loved him, although she'd fought it with everything she had. She'd been willing, for a time, to consider marrying Ralph in her effort to drive Jordan from her life. Yet even then she'd known it was useless and of course so had Ralph. Nothing could save her. Her heart had been on a collision course with Jordan's from the moment she'd been assigned the seat next to his on the flight to Hawaii.

"I'll be happy," she murmured, and then silently added *for a while.*

"So will I," Jordan said, his chest expanding with a breath and then a sigh that seemed to come all the way from his soul.

THE SMALL PRIVATE wedding took place three weeks later in Hawaii at the home of Andrew Howard. Shelly was Jill's matron of honor and Mark stood up for Jordan. Elaine Morrison, was there, too, weeping through the entire ceremony. But these weren't tears of joy. Her mother, like Jill, recognized Jordan's type and feared what it meant for her daughter's life, her happiness.

"Jill," Elaine had pleaded with her earlier that morning, before the wedding. Her eyes were filled with concern. "Are you sure this is what you want?"

Jill had nearly laughed aloud. With all her heart, with all her being, she longed to be Jordan's wife. And yet, if the opportunity had availed itself, she would have backed out of the marriage.

"He needs me." Repeatedly over the past few weeks, Jill had been reminded of how much Jordan did need her. He didn't realize it himself, of course, not on a conscious level, but something deep inside him had acknowledged his need. And in her own way, Jill needed him.

Andrew Howard had recognized the fact that they belonged together. He'd been the first one to point it out to Jill. From the time he'd been a child, Jordan's life had been devoid of love, devoid of emotion. As an adult he'd closed himself off from both, refused to allow himself to become vulnerable. That he should experience something as powerful as love for her in so short a time was something of a miracle. But then, Jill was becoming accustomed to miracles.

"All I want is your happiness," her mother had gone on to say, her eyes, so like Jill's, blurred with tears. "You're my only child. I don't want you to make the same mistakes I did."

Could loving someone ever be a mistake? Jill wondered. Her mother had loved her father, sacrificed herself for him even though, as the years went on, he'd barely seemed to reciprocate her love. And when he died prematurely, without warning, she'd become lost and miserable.

Jill knew she loved Jordan enough to put aside her fears and agree to become his wife, to bind herself in a relationship that might ultimately cause her pain. But she vowed she wouldn't lose her own identity. She wouldn't, couldn't, allow Jordan's personality to swallow her own.

He hadn't understood that in the beginning, despite her attempts to explain it. To him, Jill's desire to continue working after their marriage seemed utterly foolish. For what purpose? he'd asked. She didn't need the income; he'd made certain of that, lavishing her with gifts and more money than she could possibly spend. Her insistence on continuing her job resulted in their first real argument. But in the end Jordan had reluctantly agreed.

Andrew Howard had gone to a great deal of trouble to arrange their wedding, warming Jill's heart with his efforts. More and more she understood that the older man looked upon Jordan as the son he'd lost. He was more than a mentor, far more than a friend. He was the only real family Jordan had—until now.

Flowers filled every room of Andrew's oceanfront home, their fragrance sweet in the summer air. An archway of orange blossoms stood outside on the lush green lawn that overlooked the roaring ocean. A small reception and dinner were to follow. Tables laid with white linen tablecloths were placed around the patio.

The warm wind whispered over Jill as Andrew Howard came to escort her into the sunshine where

Jordan was waiting. Andrew paused when he saw her, his eyes vivid with appreciation. "I've never had a daughter," he said softly, "but if I did, I'd want her to be like you."

Tears of love and gratitude filled her eyes. Her mother, fussing about Jill, arranged the long, flowing train of the dress, then slowly straightened. "He's right," Elaine said softly, stepping back to examine Jill. "You've never looked more beautiful."

It was the dress, Jill realized. The dress and its magic. She ran her glove along the bodice with its Venetian lace and row upon row of delicate pearls. The high collar was adorned with pearls, too, each one stitched on by hand. The skirt flared from her waist, the hem accentuated with a flounce of lace and wide satin ribbons.

Andrew Howard stood beside her mother as the minister asked Jordan and Jill to repeat their vows. Jill's gaze met Jordan's as she made her promises. Her voice, although low, was steady and confident. Jordan's eyes held hers with a look of warmth, of tenderness.

A magic wedding dress? The scenario seemed implausible. Yet here they were, standing before God, their friends and family, declaring their love for one another.

"You look so beautiful," Shelly told Jill shortly after the ceremony. "Even more beautiful than the day you first tried on the dress."

"My hair wasn't done and I didn't have on much makeup and I—"

"No," Shelly interrupted, squeezing Jill's fingers, "it's more than that. You hadn't met Jordan yet. It's complete now."

"What is?"

"Everything," Shelly explained with characteristic ambiguity. "Aunt Milly's wedding dress, you and Jordan. Oh, Jill," she whispered, her eyes brimming with tears, "you're going to be so happy."

Jill wanted to believe that—how she wanted to believe that!—but she was afraid. So very afraid of what the future held for her and Jordan.

"I know what you're thinking," Shelly said, dabbing her eyes. "I loved Mark when I married him. I'd loved him for months, but deep down I wondered how long a marriage between us would last. We're so different."

Jill smiled to herself. Shelly was right; she and Mark were different, but they were perfectly matched, balancing each other's strengths.

"I was sure my lack of domestic skills would drive Mark to distraction, and at the same time I was convinced the way he organizes everything would kill our relationship. Did you know that man makes lists of lists? Even before I walked to the altar, I was worried that this marriage was doomed."

"It's been all right, though, hasn't it?"

Shelly smiled. "It's been so easy—love does that, you know. It takes something that's difficult and makes it feel so effortless. You'll understand what I mean in a few months."

Unfortunately Jill shared little of her friend's confidence. She was delighted that things had worked out between Shelly and Mark, but she didn't expect the same kind of happiness for her and Jordan.

"When you stop to think about it, it's not all that surprising," Shelly had gone on to say. "Take Aunt Milly and Uncle John for example. She's educated and idealistic, and John, bless his heart, was a realist and a mechanic with barely a grade-school education. Yet he was so proud of her. He loved her until the day he died."

"Mark will always love you, too," Jill said, running her hand down the satin of the wedding dress.

"Jordan feels the same way about you."

Jill's heart stopped. It hit her then, for perhaps the first time—Jordan loved her. His love was what had guided Jill through her uncertainties. It had helped her understand what had led her to this point, helped her look past her mother's tears and her own doubts.

The small reception and dinner held immediately after the ceremony featured a light, elegant meal and a warm atmosphere. Jill met several of Jordan's business associates, who seemed both surprised and pleased for them. Even the Lundquists put in a jovial appearance, although Suzi was absent.

When it came time for them to leave, Jill kissed Andrew Howard's cheek and thanked him once more. "Everything's been wonderful."

"I lost my only son," he reminded her, his eyes momentarily aged and sad. "For years I've hungered for a family. After my wife died, and before, too, I shut myself away, locked in my grief and watched the world go on without me."

"You're being hard on yourself," Jill told him. "Your work—"

"True enough," he said, cutting her off. "For a while I was able to bury myself in my company, but two years ago I realized I'd wasted too much of my life struggling with this grief. Soon afterward I decided to retire." His gaze wandered away from Jill and toward her mother, and he smiled softly. "I think the time might be right for me to make other changes, take the next step. What do you think, my dear?"

Jill smiled. Her mother needed someone like Andrew. Someone to bring the sparkle back to her eyes, to teach her that love didn't always mean pain.

"I'd forgotten what it was like to be young," he said, now smiling easily. "I've known Jordan nearly all his life. I've watched him build a name for himself and admired his cunning. He's good, Jill, damn good. But he's a man without a family, and I suspect I see a lot of myself in him. The thought of him growing old and disillusioned with life troubled me. I want him to avoid the mistakes I made."

Funny how her mother had said basically the same thing to Jill a few hours earlier. "There are certain mistakes we each have to make," Jill returned softly. "It's the only way we seem to learn, painful as it is."

"How smart you are," Andrew said, chuckling. "Much too clever for your years."

"I love him." Somehow it was important Mr. Howard know that. "I don't know if my love will make a lot of difference, but..."

"Ah, that's where you're wrong. It will change him. Love does that, my dear, and he needs you so badly."

"How can you be sure I'll have any influence over Jordan's life? I'm marrying him because I love him, but I don't expect anything to change."

"It will. Just wait and see."

"How do you know that?"

His smile came slowly, transforming his face, brightening his eyes and relaxing his mouth. "Because, my child," he said, gripping her hand in his own, "because it once transformed my life, and I'm hopeful that it will again." He glanced at her mother as he spoke, and Jill leaned over to give him another quick kiss. "Good luck," she whispered.

"Jill," Jordan called then, approaching her. "Are you ready?"

She looked at her husband of less than two hours and nodded. He was referring to their honeymoon trip, but she... she was thinking about their lives together.

"Hmm," Jill murmured as the first light of dawn crept into their hotel room. She raised her arms high above her head and yawned.

"Good morning, wife," Jordan said, kissing her ear.

"Good morning, husband."

"Did you sleep well?"

Eyes still closed, she nodded.

"Me, too."

"I was exhausted," Jill told him, smiling shyly.

"Little wonder."

Although her eyes remained closed, Jill knew Jordan was smiling. Her introduction to the physical aspect of marriage had been incredible, wonderful. Jordan was a patient and gentle lover. Jill had felt understandably nervous, but he'd been tender and reassuring.

"I didn't know it could be so good," she said, snuggling in her husband's arms.

"I didn't, either," he surprised her by saying. His lips were in her hair, his hands exploring her soft skin. "It's enough to make a husband think about wasting away the morning in bed."

"Wasting?" Jill teased, a smile lifting the corners of her mouth. "Surely I misunderstood you. The Jordan Wilcox I've met wouldn't know how to waste time."

"It all has to do with the musical rest," he said seductively. "The all-important caesura. Who would ever have guessed something so small could change a man's entire life?" He kissed her then with a hunger that moved her, then made love to her with a need that humbled her.

It was noon before they left the hotel room and one o'clock when they returned.

"Jordan," Jill said, blushing when he reached for her the moment they were alone. "It's the middle of the day."

"So?"

"So... it's indecent."

"Really?" But as he spoke, he was lowering his mouth to hers. The kiss was intoxicating, and any resistance Jill might have felt vanished like ice in the sun.

Her hands sought his neck, and she rested her palms against the corded contours of his shoulders as he kissed her again and again.

Unable to stop herself, Jill moaned softly.

Dragging his mouth from hers, he trailed kisses down the side of her neck. "There's that sight-seeing trip you wanted to take," he reminded her. "To see the pineapple and sugarcane fields."

"It's not important. We could see them another time," she offered breathlessly.

"That's not what you claimed earlier."

"I was just thinking..." She didn't get the opportunity to finish. Jordan's kiss absorbed her words and scattered the thought.

"What did you think?"

"That married people should occasionally be willing to change their plans," she managed.

Jordan chuckled, and lifting her gently into his arms, carried her to the bed. "I'm beginning to think married life is going to agree with me." His mouth found hers and gentleness gave way to urgency.

FIVE DAYS LATER, when Jordan and Jill returned to the mainland, their honeymoon over, Jill was so deeply in love with her husband she wondered why she'd ever hesitated, why she'd fought so hard against marrying him.

The first person she called when they arrived at the penthouse was Shelly. Jordan had arranged to have her things moved there while they were away. Ralph lived at her old apartment now and was elated with the extra space.

"Have you got time to meet an old friend for lunch?" Jill asked without preamble.

"Jill!" Shelly cried. "When did you get back?"

"About an hour ago." Although he hadn't said as much, she knew Jordan was dying to get to his office. "I thought I'd steal away for a few minutes and meet you."

"I'd love to see you. Just name the place and time."

Jill did, then kissed Jordan on the cheek while he was talking to his secretary on the phone in his study. He broke away, covered the mouthpiece with his hand and gave her a surprised look. "Where are you headed?"

"Out for lunch. You don't mind, do you?"

"No." But he didn't sound all that sure.

"I thought you'd want to go to the office," she explained.

"I do," he said, wrapping his arm around her waist and bringing her close to his side.

"I know, so I thought I'd meet Shelly."

He grinned, kissed her lightly and returned to his telephone conversation as though she'd already left. Jill lingered at the door, waiting for the elevator to arrive. Part of her longed to stay with him, to hold on to the happiness before it escaped, before it was dispersed by everyday tensions and demands.

"Well," Shelly said a half hour later as she slid into the restaurant booth across from Jill, "how are the newlyweds?"

"Wonderful."

"I thought you'd be more tanned."

Jill blushed; Shelly laughed and reached for her napkin. "It was the same with Mark and me. I swear we didn't leave that hotel room for three days."

"We made several short trips," Jill said, but she didn't elaborate on exactly how short their sight-seeing ventures had been.

"Married life certainly seems to agree with you."

"It's only been a week," Jill reminded her friend. "That's hardly time enough to tell."

"I knew after the first week," Shelly said confidently, her face animated by a smile. "I figured if Mark and I survived the honeymoon, our marriage had a chance. Mark wanted to honeymoon at Niagara Falls, remember?"

"And you suggested a rafting trip through the Grand Canyon." Jill smiled at the memory. Mark was looking for tradition and Shelly was seeking adventure, but in the end, they'd learned what she and Jordan had already discovered. All that mattered was their marriage, their love for each other.

"We couldn't agree," Shelly continued. "I was seriously worried about it. If we were at odds over a honeymoon site, then what on earth would happen

when it came to dealing with the really important issues?''

Jill understood what Shelly meant. She loved Jordan; of that there could be no doubt. Now she had to
place her trust in their love, hope that it was strong
enough to withstand day-to-day reality. She was still
fearful, but ready to fight for her marriage, to keep it
safe.

Suddenly Shelly set aside the menu, pressed her
hand against her stomach and slowly exhaled.

"Shell, what's wrong?"

Shelly briefly closed her eyes. "Nothing bad. I just
can't stand to read about food."

"About food?" That made absolutely no sense to
Jill.

"I'm two months pregnant."

"Shelly!" Jill was so excited she nearly toppled her
water glass. "Why didn't you say something sooner?
Good grief, I'm your best friend—I'd think you'd
want me to know."

"I do, but I couldn't tell you until I knew, could I?"

"You just found out?"

"Not exactly." Shelly reached for a small packet of
soda crackers, tore away the cellophane wrapper and
munched on one. "I found out just before your wedding, but I didn't want to say anything then."

Jill appreciated Shelly's considerateness, her wish
not to compete with Jill's important day.

"Actually, it was Mark who told me. Imagine a
husband explaining the facts of life to his wife. I'm

such a scatterbrain—I miscalculated and didn't even know it.''

As far as Jill was concerned, this baby certainly wasn't a mistake, and from Shelly's happy glow, her friend felt the same way.

'' "I was a bit afraid Mark might be upset. Naturally we'd talked about starting a family, but neither of us planned to have it happen so soon."

"He wasn't upset, though, was he?" Jill would have been very surprised if Mark had been anything but thrilled.

"Not in the least. When he first told me what he suspected, I just laughed." She shook her head in mock consternation. "You'd think I'd know better than to question a man who sleeps with his Daily Planner by his side!"

"I'm so excited for you."

"Now that I've adjusted to it, I can't wait. I have to admit, though, this baby's a real surprise."

After the waitress had taken their order, Jill relaxed against the banquette cushion. "It happened just the way you said it would," she said.

"What did?"

"Loving Jordan." Jill felt a little shy talking so openly about something so intimate. Although she and Jordan were married and deeply in love with each other, they never spoke of their feelings. Jordan was still uncomfortable with expressing emotion. But he didn't need to tell Jill he loved her, not when he went about proving it in every way he knew how. She'd never pressured him, never demanded the words.

"The day we were married you told me love makes the difficult things seem effortless. Remember?"

Ever confident, Shelly grinned. "You're going to be so happy..." She paused, swallowed and reached for her napkin, dabbing her eyes. "I get so emotional these days, I can't believe it. The other night I found myself weeping at a stupid television commercial."

"You?"

"If you think that's bad, Mark's got a terrible case of morning sickness."

Jill laughed at her friend's teasing. Laughter came easily since her marriage; it was all the happiness in her heart brimming over, spilling out. She'd never felt so carefree or laughed at so many silly things before.

When Jill returned from lunch two hours later, Jordan was gone. Exhausted from the flight and the excitement of the past week, she crawled into bed and slept, waking when it was dark.

Rolling onto her back, she stretched luxuriously under the weight of the blanket and smiled, musing how thoughtful it was of Jordan to let her sleep.

She kicked aside the blanket and blindly sent her feet searching for her shoes. Yawning, she walked into the living room, surprised to find it dark.

"Jordan?" she called.

She was greeted by silence.

Turning on the lights, Jill was shocked to discover it was after nine. Jordan must still be at the office, she supposed, her stomach knotting. Could it be happening so soon? Could he have grown tired of her already?

No sooner had the thought formed when the elevator doors opened and Jordan appeared. She didn't fly into his arms, although that was her first instinct.

"Hello," she greeted him, a bit coolly.

He was loosening his tie. "What time is it?"

"Nine-fifteen. Are you hungry?"

He paused, as though he needed to think about it. "Yeah, I guess I am. Sorry I didn't call. I didn't have a clue it was this late."

"No problem."

He followed her into the kitchen and slid his arms around her waist while she investigated the contents of the refrigerator.

"It won't be like this every night," he said, his words sounding very much like a promise her father had once made to her mother.

"I know," Jill said, desperately trying to sound as though she believed him.

SHE COULDN'T SLEEP that night. Perhaps it was the long nap she'd taken in the middle of the afternoon; at least that was what she tried to tell herself. More likely, though, it was the gnawing fear that Jordan's love for her was already faltering. She tried to push the doubts aside, tried to convince herself she was overreacting. He'd been away from his office for a week. There must have been all kinds of important issues that demanded his attention. Was she expecting too much?

In the morning, she promised herself, she'd talk to him about it. But when she awoke, Jordan had already left for the office. At least that was where she assumed he'd gone.

Frowning, she dressed and wandered into the kitchen for a cup of coffee.

"Morning." Jordan's cook, Mrs. Murphy, a middle-aged woman with sparkling blue eyes and a wide smile, greeted her. Jill smiled back, although her cheerfulness felt a little strained.

"Hello, Mrs. Murphy, it's nice to see you again," she said, helping herself to coffee. "Uh, what time did Mr. Wilcox leave this morning?"

"Early," the cook said with a disappointed sigh. "I was thinking Mr. Wilcox would stop working so hard once he was married. He hasn't even been home from his honeymoon twenty-four hours and he's already at the office at the crack of dawn."

Jill hated to disillusion the woman, but this wasn't Jordan's first trip to his office. "I'll see what I can do to give him some incentive to stay home," Jill said, savoring the first sip of her coffee.

Mrs. Murphy chuckled. "I'm glad to hear it. That man works too many hours. I've been telling my George for some time now that Mr. Wilcox needs a wife to keep him home at night."

"I'll do my best," Jill promised, but she had the distinct feeling her efforts would make little difference. Checking her watch, she quickly drank the rest of her coffee and hurried into the bedroom to shower.

Within half an hour she was dressed and ready for work.

"Mrs. Murphy," she told the cook, "I'll be at work—PayRite Pharmacy—if Jordan happens to call. Tell him I'll be home a little after five." Jill wished she'd had the chance to talk to him herself; she was more than a little distressed that within a week of their wedding she was communicating with her husband through a third party.

Despite everything, Jill enjoyed her day, which was busier than usual. The pharmacy staff took her out for a celebration lunch, and dozens of customers came by to wish her well. Many of the people whose prescriptions she filled regularly had become friends. In light of how her married life was working out, Jill was thankful she'd decided to keep her job.

By five she was eager to return home, eager to share her day with Jordan and hear about his. She was met by the aroma of cheese, tomato sauce and garlic, and followed it into the kitchen, where she found Mrs. Murphy untying her apron.

"Whatever you're cooking smells sinfully delicious."

"It's my lasagna. Mr. Wilcox's favorite."

Jill opened the oven door and peeked inside. She was famished. "Did Jordan phone?" she asked, her voice rising on a note of longing.

"About fifteen minutes ago. I told him you'd be home a bit after five."

No sooner were the words out than the phone rang. Jill was licking spicy tomato sauce from her fingertip when she answered.

"This is Brian Macauley, Mr. Wilcox's assistant," a crisp male voice informed her. "He's asked that I let you know he won't be home for dinner."

CHAPTER NINE

"JILL."

Her name seemed to come from a long way off. Someone was calling her, but she could barely hear.

"Sweetheart." The voice was louder now.

She snuggled into the warmth, ignoring the persistent sound. After hours and hours of forcing herself to stay awake, she'd finally given up the effort and succumbed to the sweet seduction of sleep.

"Honey, if you don't wake up, you'll get a crick in your neck."

"Jordan?" Her eyes instantly flew open to find her husband kneeling on the carpet beside her chair. She straightened and stared at him as though seeing him for the first time. "Oh, Jordan," she whispered, wrapping her arms around his neck. "I'm so glad you're home."

"With this kind of reception, I'll have to stay away more often."

Jill decided to ignore that comment. "What time is it?"

"Late," was all he said.

She kissed him, needing him, savoring the feel of his arms around her. He looked dreadful. He hadn't been home for dinner in well over a week and spent all hours of the day and night at his office.

Although she'd asked him several times, Jordan's only explanation was that a project he'd been working on had gone wrong. A project. For this he was willing to send both their lives into tumult; for this he was willing to place their marriage at risk. The upheaval had all but ruined the memory of their brief idyllic honeymoon. They'd been back in Seattle two weeks now, and Jill hadn't been allotted a single uninterrupted hour of Jordan's time.

"Are you hungry?" She doubted he'd eaten a decent meal in days.

He shook his head, then rubbed his face wearily. "I'm more tired than anything."

"How much longer is this going to continue?" she asked, keeping her voice as steady as she could. She'd gone into this marriage with her eyes wide open. From the moment she'd met Jordan, she'd known how stiff the competition would be, how demanding his way of life was. She'd always known how difficult keeping their marriage intact was going to be. But she'd figured their love would hold the edge for at least the first couple of years.

Unfortunately she'd figured wrong. If anything, she'd underestimated the strength of his obsession with business and success. Jordan loved her; he might rarely have told her that, but Jill didn't need the words. What she did need was some of his time, some of his attention.

"I've barely seen you all week," she reminded him. "You're gone before I wake up in the mornings. Heaven only knows what time you get home at night."

"It won't be much longer," Jordan said stiffly, standing. "I promise."

"Would it be so terrible if this project folded?"

"Yes," he returned emphatically.

"One failure isn't the end of the world, you know."

Jordan smiled wryly, and his condescension angered her.

"It's true," she answered softly. "Did I ever tell you about trying out for the lead in the high-school play during my senior year?"

Jordan frowned. "No, but is this another story like the one about your piano-playing?"

Jill tucked her legs under her and rested one elbow on the chair arm. "A little."

Jordan sank down on the leather sofa across from her, leaned his head back and closed his eyes. "In that case, why don't you move directly to the point and skip the story?"

He wasn't being rude, Jill told herself, only practical. He was exhausted and in desperate need of rest. He didn't have the energy to wade through her mournful tale in search of a moral.

"All right," she agreed amicably enough. "You've probably already guessed I didn't get the lead. But I'd been so sure I would. I'd played major roles in several plays. In fact, I'd gotten every part I'd ever tried out for. Not only didn't I get this part, I wasn't even in the play, and damn it all, even now I think I would have done a really good job of playing Helen Keller."

He grinned. "I'm sure you would have, too."

"What I learned most from that experience was not to fear failure. I survived not playing Helen Keller, and later, in college, when I was awarded a wonderful role, it heightened my appreciation of that success." When Jordan didn't immediately respond, she added, "Do you understand what I'm saying, or are you asleep?"

His eyes were closed but his mouth lifted in a gentle smile. "I was just mulling over the sad history of your musical and acting careers."

Jill smiled, too. "I know it sounds ludicrous, but failure liberated me. My heart and soul went into my audition for that role, and when I lost, I felt I could never act again. It took me a long time to regain my confidence, to be willing to hazard another rejection, but eventually I was stronger for it. When I decided to try out for a play in my freshman year of college, I felt as though I was somehow protected, because failure wasn't going to rock me the way it had earlier."

"So you wanted to be an actress?"

"No, I'm not much good at waiting tables."

It took Jordan a moment to catch her joke, but when he did, he laughed out loud.

"You know what they say about hindsight being twenty-twenty? In this case it's true. If failure hadn't taught me to appreciate success when I had it, I might have fallen into a nasty trap."

"What was that?"

"Thinking I deserved it, believing I was so talented, so incredibly gifted, so good that I'd never lose."

Jordan fell silent. Jill waited a moment, then said, "Mr. Howard told me something . . . about the shopping-mall project. I didn't say anything to you at the time because . . . well, because I wasn't sure he wanted me to."

She had Jordan's full attention now.

He straightened, his eyes searching hers. "What did he say?"

"He hasn't often gone in on a construction project with you, has he?"

"Only a handful of times."

"There's a reason for that."

"Oh?"

"You've never failed."

Jordan's head came up sharply. "I beg your pardon?"

Jill realized Jordan found such thinking preposterous. If anything, his successes should have been an inducement to his financial supporters.

"Mr. Howard explained that he doesn't like to deal with a man until he's been devastated financially at least once."

"That makes no sense," Jordan returned irritably.

"Perhaps not. Since my experience in the financial world is limited to balancing my checkbook, I wouldn't know," Jill admitted.

"Who's going to lend money to someone who's failed?"

"Apparently Andrew Howard," Jill said with a grin. "He told me the man who's lost everything is much more careful the next time around."

"I didn't realize you and Howard talked business."

"We didn't." She did her best to appear nonchalant. "Mostly we discussed you."

This didn't please Jordan, either. "I'd prefer to think I owe my success to hard work, determination and foresight. I certainly couldn't have come as far as I have without them."

"True enough," Jill agreed willingly, "but..."

"Is there always going to be a but?"

She nodded, trying to hold back a laugh. Actually she was enjoying this, while her tired husband was left to suffer the indignities of her insights.

"Well," he said shortly, "go on, knock my argument all to hell."

"Oh, I agree your intelligence and dedication have played a large role in your success, but others have worked just as hard, been just as determined and shown just as much foresight—and lost everything."

Jordan scowled. "My, you're full of good cheer, aren't you?"

"I just don't want you to put so much store in this one project. If it falls apart, so what? You're beating yourself to death with this." She didn't mention what it was doing to their marriage; that went without saying.

He considered her words for a few seconds, then his face tightened. "I won't lose. I absolutely, categorically, refuse not to succeed."

"How much longer?" Jill asked when she could disguise the defeat and frustration she was feeling.

He hesitated, then massaged the back of his neck as though to ease away a tiredness that stretched from the top of his head to the bottom of his feet. "A week. It shouldn't take much longer than that."

A week. Seven days. She closed her eyes, because looking at him, seeing him this exhausted, this spent, was painful. He needed her support now, not her censure.

"All right," she murmured.

"I don't like this any better than you do." Jordan stood and wrapped her securely in his embrace, burying his face in the warm curve of her neck. "I'm a newlywed, remember. There's no one I want to spend time with more than my wife."

Jill nodded, because it would have been impossible to speak.

"I wish you hadn't waited up for me," he said, lifting her into his arms and carrying her into their bedroom. Without turning on the light, he settled her on the bed and lay down beside her, placing his head on her chest. Jill's fingers idly stroked his hair.

Words burned in her throat, the need to unburden herself, but she dared not. Jordan was exhausted. This wasn't the right time. Would it ever be the right time?

There had been so many lonely evenings, so many empty mornings. Every night Jill went to bed alone, and only when Jordan slipped in beside her did she feel alive. Only when they were together did she feel whole. And so she waited night after night for a few precious minutes, knowing they were all he had to spare.

The even sound of Jordan's breathing told her he'd fallen asleep already. The weight on her chest was growing uncomfortable, yet she continued to stroke his hair for several minutes, unwilling to disturb his rest.

She'd always known it would come to this; she just hadn't expected it to happen so soon. A week. He'd promised her it would be over within a week.

And it would be—until the next time.

JILL AWOKE EARLY the following morning, amazed to find Jordan asleep beside her. At some point during the night he'd rolled away from her and covered them both with a blanket. He hadn't bothered to undress.

Jill wriggled toward him and playfully kissed his ear. She knew she ought to let him sleep, but she also knew he'd be annoyed if he was late for the office.

Slowly he opened his eyes, looking surprised to find her there with him.

"Morning," she whispered, with a series of tiny, nibbling kisses.

"What time is it?" he asked.

"Somewhere around eight, I'd guess." She looped her arms around his neck and smiled down at him.

"Hmm. An indecent hour."

"Very indecent."

"My favorite time of day." His fingers were busy unfastening the opening of her pajama top and his eyes blazed with unmistakable need.

"Jordan," she said a bit breathlessly, "you'll be late for work."

A smile coaxed his mouth. "I fully intend to be," he said, directing her lips to his.

"IT'S HAPPENING ALREADY, isn't it?" Elaine Morrison said bluntly the following Saturday. She stood in Jill's living room, holding a china cup and saucer and staring out the window. The view of the Olympic Mountains was spectacular, the white peaks jutting against a backdrop of bright blue sky as fluffy clouds drifted past.

Jill knew precisely what her mother was saying. She responded the only way she could—truthfully. "Yes."

Elaine turned, her face pale, haunted with the pain of the past, the pain she saw reflected in her daughter's life. "I feared this would happen."

Until recently, Jill had found communicating with her mother difficult. After her husband's death, Elaine had withdrawn from life, hidden herself away in her grief and regrets. In many ways, Jill had lost her mother at the same time as she had her father.

"Mom, it's all right," Jill said in an attempt to reassure her. "It's only for the next little while. Once this project's under control everything will be different."

Jill knew better. She wasn't fooling herself, and she sincerely doubted she'd be able to fool her mother.

"I warned you," Elaine said, walking to the white leather sofa and sitting tensely on the edge. Placing the cup and saucer on a nearby table, she turned pleading eyes to Jill. "Didn't I tell you? The day of the wedding—I knew then."

"Yes, Mother, you warned me."

"Why didn't you listen?"

Jill exhaled slowly, praying for patience. "I'm in love with him, just like you loved Daddy."

It seemed unfair to drag her father into this, her much-grieved father, but it was the only way Jill knew to explain.

"What are you going to do about it?"

"Mother," Jill sighed. "It's not as though Jordan's having an affair."

"He might as well be," Elaine replied heatedly. "Here it is, Saturday afternoon and he's working. One look at him told me he had the same drive and ambition, the same need for power, as your father."

"Mother, please... It isn't like that with Jordan."

The older woman's eyes were infinitely sad as she gazed at her daughter. "Don't count on that, Jill. Just don't count on it."

HER MOTHER'S VISIT had unsettled Jill. Afterward, she tried to relax with a book, but found her concentration wandering. The phone rang at six, just as it had every night that week. Jordan's secretary or assistant had called to let her know Jordan wouldn't be home for dinner.

One ring.

Walking over to the phone, Jill stood directly in front of it, but she didn't lift the receiver.

Two rings.

Drawing in a deep breath, she flexed her fingers. Twice in the past couple of weeks, Jordan had phoned himself. Maybe he'd be on the other end of the line, inviting her to join him for dinner. Maybe he was phoning to tell her he'd unscrambled the entire mess and he'd be home within the next half hour. Perhaps he was calling to suggest they take a few days off and vacation somewhere exotic, just the two of them.

Three rings.

Jill could feel her pulse throbbing at the base of her throat. But still she didn't answer.

Four rings.

Five rings.

The phone went silent.

Her entire body was trembling when she turned away and walked toward the bedroom. She sat on the bed and covered her face with both hands.

The phone began to ring again, the sound reverberating loudly through the apartment. Jill slapped her hands over her ears, unable to bear it. Each ring tormented her, pretending to offer her hope when there was none. It wouldn't be Jordan, but his assistant, and his message would be the same one he'd relayed every night that week.

Making a rapid decision, Jill reached for her jacket and purse and hurried toward the penthouse elevator.

Not having anywhere in particular to go, she wandered downtown until she found a movie theater. The movie wasn't one that really interested her, but she bought a ticket, anyway, willing to subject herself to a B-grade comedy if it meant she could escape for a couple of hours.

Actually the movie turned out to be quite entertaining. The plot was ridiculous, but there were enough humorous moments to make her laugh. And if Jill had ever needed some comic relief, it was now.

On impulse she stopped at a deli and picked up a couple of sandwiches, then flagged down a taxi. Before she could change her mind, she gave the driver the address of Jordan's office.

She had a bit of trouble convincing the security guard to admit her, but eventually, after the guard talked to Jordan, she was allowed in the building.

"Jill," he snapped when she stepped off the elevator, "where have you been?"

"It's good to see you, too," she said, ignoring the irritation in his voice. She kissed his cheek, then walked casually past him.

"Where were you?"

"I went out to a movie," she said, strolling into his office. His desk, a large mahogany one, was littered with folders and papers. She noted dryly that he was alone. Everyone else had taken the weekend off, but he hadn't afforded himself the same luxury.

"You were at a movie?"

She didn't bother to answer. "I thought you might be hungry," she said, neatly stacking a pile of folders in order to clear one small corner of his desk. "I stopped in at Griffin's and bought us both something to eat."

"I ate earlier."

"Oh." So much for that brilliant idea. "Unfortunately, I didn't." She plopped herself down in the comfortable leather chair and pulled a turkey-on-rye from the sack, along with a cup of coffee, setting both on the small space she'd cleared.

Jordan looked as though he wasn't sure what to do with her. He leaned over the desk and shoved several files to one side.

"I'm not interrupting anything, am I?"

"Of course not," he answered dryly. "I was staying late for the fun of it."

"There certainly isn't any reason to hurry home," she returned just as dryly.

Jordan rubbed his eyes, and his shoulders slumped. "I'm sorry, Jill. These past couple of weeks have been hard on you, haven't they?"

He moved behind her and grasped her shoulders. His touch had always had a calming effect on Jill, and she wanted to fight it, wanted to fight her weakness for him.

"Jill," Jordan whispered. "Let's go home." He bent down then and kissed the side of her neck. A shiver raced down her body and Jill breathed deeply, placing her hands on his.

"Home," she repeated softly, as if it was the most beautiful word in the English language.

"JILL," SHELLY CRIED, her eyes widening when she opened the front door, one evening a few weeks later. "What's wrong?"

"Wrong," Jill repeated numbly.

"You look awful."

"How kind of you to point it out."

"I've got it," Shelly said excitedly, tapping her fingers against her lips, "you're pregnant, too."

"Unfortunately, no," she said, passing Shelly and walking into the kitchen. She took a clean mug from the dishwasher and poured herself a cup of coffee. "How are you feeling, by the way?"

"Rotten," Shelly admitted wryly, then added with a smile, "Wonderful."

Jill pulled out a kitchen chair and sat down. If she spent another evening alone, she was going to go crazy. She probably should have phoned Shelly first rather than dropping in unannounced, but driving over here gave her an excuse to leave the penthouse. This evening she badly needed an excuse. Anything to get away. Anything to escape the loneliness. Funny, she'd lived on her own for years, yet she'd never felt so empty, so alone, as she had in the past two months. Even the conversation with Andrew Howard earlier in the evening had only momentarily lifted her spirits.

"Where's Mark?"

Shelly grinned. "You won't believe it if I tell you."

"Tell me."

"He's taking a carpentry class."

"Carpentry? Mark?"

Shelly's grin broadened. "He wants to make a cradle for the baby. He's so sweet I can barely stand it. You know Mark, he's absolutely useless when it comes to anything practical. Give him a few numbers and he's a whiz kid, but when he has to change a light bulb, he needs an instruction manual. I love him dearly, but when he announced he was going to build a cradle for the baby, I couldn't help it, I laughed.''

"Shelly!"

"I know. It was a rotten thing to do, so Mark's out there proving how wrong I am. This is his first night, and I just hope to heaven the instructor doesn't kick him out of class."

Despite her unhappiness, Jill smiled. It felt good to be around Shelly, to laugh again, to have reason to laugh.

"I haven't talked to you in ages," Shelly remarked, stirring her coffee. "But then I shouldn't expect to, should I? You and Jordan are still on your honeymoon, aren't you?"

Tears sprang instantly to Jill's eyes, blurring her vision. "Yes," she lied, looking away, praying that Shelly, who was so happy in her own marriage, wouldn't notice how miserable Jill was in hers.

"Oh, before I forget," Shelly said excitedly, "I heard from Aunt Milly."

"What did she have to say?"

"She asked me to thank you for your letter, telling her about meeting Jordan and everything. She loves a good romance. Then she said something odd."

"Oh?"

"She felt the dress was meant to be worn one more time."

"Again? By who?"

Shelly leaned forward, cupping her mug with both hands. "I realize you and Jordan were too wrapped up in each other on your wedding day to notice, but your mother and Mr. Howard got along famously. Milly wouldn't have known that, of course, but ... it's obviously meant to be."

"My mother." Now that she recalled her conversation with Andrew at the wedding, it made sense. In the weeks since their return from Hawaii, she'd forgotten about it. He'd phoned Jill twice since the wedding, but he hadn't mentioned Elaine; nor had her mother mentioned him.

"What do you think?"

"My mother and Mr. Howard?" Jill felt an immense sense of rightness.

"Isn't that incredible?" Shelly positively beamed. "Wonderful?" Until recently—the arrival of the wedding dress, to be exact—Jill hadn't realized what a complete romantic her friend was.

"But Mom hasn't said a word."

"Did you expect her to?"

Jill shrugged. For a lot of reasons, Shelly was right. Elaine would approach romance and remarriage with extreme caution.

"Wouldn't it be fabulous if your mother ended up wearing the dress?"

Jill nodded and, placing her fingertips to her temple, closed her eyes. "A vision's coming to me now..."

Shelly laughed.

"I think we should call my mom and tell her that we both had a clear vision of her standing in the dress next to a distinguished-looking older man."

Once again, Shelly giggled. "Oh, that's good. That's really good." She sighed contentedly. "The dress definitely belongs with your mother, you know. We'll have to do something about that soon."

Jill pretended her tears were ones of mirth and dashed them away with the back of one hand.

But the amusement slowly faded from Shelly's eyes. "Are you going to tell me what's wrong, or are you going to make me torture it out of you?"

"I—I'm fine."

"No, you're not. Don't forget I know you. You've been my best friend for years. You wouldn't be here if something wasn't wrong."

"It's that crazy wedding dress again," Jill confessed.

"The wedding dress?"

"I should never have worn it."

"Jill!" Shelly exclaimed, then frowned. "You're not making any sense."

"It clouded my judgment. I was always the romantic one, remember? Always a sucker for a good love story. When Milly first mailed you the dress, I thought it was the neatest thing to happen since low-fat ice cream."

"Not true! Remember how you persuaded me—"

"I know what I said," Jill interrupted. "But deep down inside I could hardly wait to see what happened. When you and Mark decided to marry, I was thrilled. Later, after I arrived in Hawaii and you had the wedding dress delivered to me, I kind of allowed myself to play along with the fantasy—until I met

Jordan, that is. I've wanted to get married for a long time. I'd like to have several children."

"Jill," Shelly said, looking puzzled, "I'm not sure I follow you."

"I think I might have even felt a little bit...jealous that you got married before I did. I was the one who wanted a husband, not you, and yet here you were so deeply in love with Mark. Somehow it just didn't seem fair." The tears slipped down her cheek and she absently brushed them aside.

"But you're married now and Jordan's crazy about you."

"He was for about a week, but that's worn off."

"He loves you!"

"Yes, I suppose in his own way he does." Jill hadn't the strength to argue. "But not enough."

"Not enough?"

"It's too difficult to explain," she said, swallowing the tears that clogged her throat. "I came over to tell you I've made a decision." As hard as she tried, she couldn't keep herself from sobbing, "I've decided to leave Jordan."

CHAPTER TEN

SHELLY'S EYES NARROWED with disbelief. "You can't possibly mean that!"

Leaving Jordan wasn't a decision Jill had made lightly. She'd agonized over it for days. Unable to answer her friend, she pushed back her hair with hands that refused to stop shaking. Her stomach was in knots. "It just isn't going to work. I need some time away from him to sort through my feelings. I don't want to leave, but I'm afraid I'll just fall apart if I stay any longer."

Shelly never had been one to disguise her feelings. Anger flashed from her eyes like blue fire. "You haven't even given the marriage a decent chance. It hasn't even been two months."

"I know everything I need to know. Jordan isn't married to me, he's married to his company. Shelly, you're my best friend—but there are things you don't know, things I can't explain about what's happening between me and Jordan. Things that go back to my childhood and being raised the way I was."

"You love him."

Jill closed her eyes and nodded. She did love Jordan, so much her heart was breaking, so much she didn't know if she'd survive leaving him, so much she doubted she'd ever love this deeply again.

"I don't expect you to understand," Jill continued, choking over the words. "I wanted you to know...because I'm going to be living with my mother for a while. Just until I can sort through my feelings and make a decision."

"Have you told him yet?" Shelly's voice sounded less sharp.

"No." Jill had delayed that as long as possible, not knowing what to say or how to say it. This wasn't a game, or an attempt to manipulate Jordan into devoting more time to her and their marriage. She refused to fall into that trap. If she was going to make the break, she wanted it to be clean. Decisive. Not cluttered with threats.

"You *are* going to tell him?"

"Of course." She could never be so cowardly as to move out while Jordan was at the office. Besides, the sorry truth was that she might be gone for days before he noticed.

Confronting him wasn't a task she relished. She knew Jordan well and could predict his reaction—he'd be furious with her, more than she'd probably ever seen him. Jill was prepared for that. But in the end he would let her go as if she meant nothing to him. His pride would demand that.

"When do you plan to tell him?" Shelly asked softly, seeming to understand for the first time Jill's torment. A true sign of the strength of their friendship was that Shelly didn't ply her with questions, but accepted Jill's less-than-satisfactory explanation.

"Tonight." She hadn't packed her things yet, but she intended to do that when she got back home.

Home.

The word echoed in her mind. Although the penthouse was so distinctly marked with Jordan's personality, it did feel like home. She'd only lived there a short while, but in the long, lonely weeks following her honeymoon with Jordan, she'd become intimately acquainted with every room. She was going to miss the solace she gained from looking out over Puget Sound and the jagged peaks of the Olympics. And Mrs. Murphy had become a special friend, almost like a second mother, who fretted over her and worried about the long hours Jordan worked. Jill would miss her, too. Although Jill hadn't mentioned leaving to the cook, she guessed that Mrs. Murphy wouldn't be surprised.

"You're sure this is what you want?" Shelly asked regretfully.

Leaving Jordan, even for a short time, was the last thing Jill wanted. Yet it had to be done—and soon, before it was too late, before she found it impossible to go.

"Don't answer that," Shelly whispered. "The pain in your eyes says everything I need to know."

Jill stood and searched in her purse for a tissue. The tears were rolling freely down her cheeks now. She had to compose herself before she encountered Jordan.

Had to draw on every bit of inner strength she possessed.

Shelly hugged her, and once again Jill was grateful for their friendship. They were as close as sisters, and Jill had never needed family more than she did right then.

The penthouse echoed with an empty silence when she arrived home. Jill stood in the middle of the living room, then slowly moved around, skimming her hand over each piece of furniture. Her gaze gravitated toward the view, and she walked toward the window, staring into the night. Far below, lights flashed and glowed, but she was far removed from the brilliance. Far removed from the light . . .

Reluctantly, she entered the bedroom she shared with Jordan. Her breath came in shallow, pain-filled gasps as she dragged out her suitcases and set them on top of the bed. Carefully, she folded her clothes and one by one deposited them inside.

Several times she was forced to stop, clenching an article of clothing in her hands, crushing the fabric, until she composed herself enough to continue. Tears stung her eyes, but she refused to succumb to them. If ever there was a time she needed to be strong, it was now.

"Jill?"

Her hands froze. Her heart froze. She hadn't expected Jordan to come home for several hours yet. They'd barely seen one another all week, barely spoken.

"Where are you going?" he asked calmly.

Pulling herself together, Jill turned to face him. Jordan stood on the other side of the room, but he might as well have been half a world away. He held himself stiffly, his gaze perplexed.

"My mother's," she finally answered.

"Is she ill?"

"No..." Drawing a deep breath, hoping it would calm her frantic heart, she forged ahead. "I'm leaving for a while. I—I need to sort through my feelings...make some important decisions."

The fire that leapt into his eyes was filled with anger. "You plan to divorce me?" he demanded incredulously.

"No. For now, I'm just moving in with my mother."

"Why?"

Jill could feel her own anger mounting. "That you even have to ask should be answer enough! Can't you see what's happening? Don't you care? At this rate our marriage isn't going to last another month." She paused to gulp a much-needed breath. "My instincts told me this would happen, but I was so much in love with you that I chose to ignore what was obvious from the first. You don't need a wife. You never have. I don't understand why you wanted to marry me because—"

"When did all this come on?" he growled.

"It's been coming on, as you say, from the minute we got home from our honeymoon. Our marriage has to be one of the shortest on record. One week. That's all the time you allotted to it. I need more than five minutes at the end of the day when you're so exhausted you can hardly speak. I wish I were stronger, but I'm not. I need more from you than you can give me."

"You might have said something to me earlier."

"I did a hundred times."

"When?" he barked.

"I'm not going to get involved in a shouting match with you, Jordan. I refuse to sit by and watch you work yourself to death over some stupid project. You'd said ages ago that it'd be finished in a week. I was stupid enough to believe you. If it's so important to you that you're willing to risk everything to keep it from folding, then fine, it's all yours."

"When did you tell me?" he demanded a second time.

"Do you remember our conversation last night?" she asked starkly.

Jordan frowned, then shook his head.

"I didn't think you had."

The previous afternoon, Jill had been so terribly lonely that she'd reached for the phone, planning to call Ralph to invite him to a movie. She'd nearly dialed his number before she remembered she was married. The incident had had a profound effect upon her. She didn't *feel* married. She felt abandoned. Forgotten. Unimportant. If she was going to live her life alone, then fine, she could accept that. But she refused to be a pretty bird locked in a cage and brought out and stroked when it was convenient.

This time apart would help her gain perspective, show her what she needed to do. Explaining it to Jordan was impossible, though. But in time, a week perhaps, she might be able to tell him all that was in her heart.

"What was it you said last night?" Jordan wanted to know, clearly confused.

Jill neatly folded a silk blouse and put it inside the suitcase. "I told you how I almost called Ralph to ask him if he wanted to see a movie . . . and you laughed. Remember? You found it humorous that your wife would forget she was a married woman. What you apparently didn't understand was what had led me to the point of wanting to call an old boyfriend."

"You're not making a damn bit of sense."

"No, I suppose not. I'm sorry, Jordan. I wish I could explain it better. But as I already told you, I need more from our relationship than you can give me . . ."

"I've explained that this project would be settled soon. I'll grant you it's taking longer than I'd thought, but if you'd just be patient for a little longer . . . Is that so much to ask? You'd think . . ." He hesitated, then jammed his hands in his pockets and marched to the other side of the room. "These past few weeks haven't been a picnic for me, either. You'd think a wife would be more willing to lend her husband support, instead of bullying him into doing what she wants with threats."

It didn't surprise Jill that Jordan assumed her leaving was merely a ploy. He didn't understand how serious she was.

"I can't live like this. I just can't!" she cried. "Not now, not ever. I want my children to know their father! My own was a shadow who passed through my life, and I couldn't bear my children to suffer what I did."

"This is a fine time for you to figure it all out," Jordan growled, his hold on his frustration and anger obviously precarious.

"If I could go back and change everything, I would...I would." Hurrying now, she closed her suitcases.

"Are you pregnant?" The question came at her like a bolt of lightning.

"No."

"You're sure?"

"Of course."

A moment of silence followed as she collected her purse and a sweater.

"Nothing I can say is going to change your mind, is it?"

"No." She reached for the handles of the two suitcases and dragged them both across the bed. "If...if there's any reason you need to get hold of me, I'll be at my mother's."

Jordan just stood there, his back toward her, his spine ramrod stiff. "If you're so set on leaving, then just go."

"JILL, SWEETHEART." Her mother knocked lightly, then walked into the darkening bedroom. Jill sat on the padded window seat, her knees tucked under her chin, staring out the bay window to the oak-lined street below. Often as a child she'd sat there and reflected on her problems. But now her problems couldn't be worked out by staring out her bedroom window or by pounding on a piano for an hour or two.

"How are you feeling?"

"Fine." She wasn't ready to talk yet.

"I've made dinner," Elaine told her, her voice gentle and sympathetic. There was a radiant glow about her these days. Andrew Howard had called almost daily since Jill had been living with her mother, although he knew nothing of her separation from Jordan. Jill had sworn her mother to secrecy. The last Jill heard, Andrew planned to fly to the mainland early the next month so that he and Elaine could spend some time together. Jill was delighted for her mother and for Andrew. Her own situation, though, was bleak.

"Thanks, Mom, but I'm not hungry."

Her mother didn't argue, but sat on the edge of the cushion and leaned forward to hug Jill. The unexpected display of affection moved Jill to tears.

"You haven't eaten anything to speak of all week."

"I'm fine, Mom." Jill didn't want her mother fussing over her just now, and she was grateful when her mother seemed to realize it. Elaine lovingly brushed the hair from Jill's face and got to her feet.

"If you need me..."

"I'm fine, Mom."

Her mother hesitated. "Are you going back to him, Jill?"

Jill didn't answer. Not because she didn't want to, but because she didn't know. She hadn't heard from Jordan at all in the week she'd been gone. A concerned Shelly had dropped by twice, unobtrusively leaving the wedding dress, in its original mailing box, on Jill's window seat. Even Ralph had called. But she hadn't heard from Jordan.

She shouldn't miss him this much. Shouldn't feel so empty without him, so lost. Jill had hoped this time apart would clear her thoughts. It hadn't. If anything they were more confused than ever. Her musings were like snagged fishing lines, impossible to untangle, frustrating her more by the hour.

She hadn't really expected him to get in touch with her, but deep down she'd hoped. Foolishly hoped. Although if he had, Jill didn't know how she would have reacted.

The doorbell chimed in the distance. A few moments later Jill heard her mother talking with another woman. The voice wasn't familiar and Jill pressed her forehead to her knees, suddenly weary. Part of her had wanted the visitor to be Jordan. Fool that she was, Jill prayed that he'd be willing to put aside his pride enough to come after her, to convince her they could make their marriage work. Her heart ached for the sight of him. Obviously, though, any move would have to come from her. But Jill wasn't ready. Not yet. Not when her heart was in such turmoil.

"Jill?" Her mother knocked lightly again on her bedroom door and opened it a crack. "There's someone here to see you. A Suzi Lundquist. She says it's important."

"Suzi Lundquist?" Jill repeated incredulously.

"She's waiting for you in the living room," her mother said.

Jill hadn't the slightest idea why Suzi would want to see her. Jordan had used her to ward off the younger woman's affections. Perhaps Suzi still loved Jordan and intended to rekindle the fire. But in that case, she wasn't likely to announce her plans to Jill.

Slipping into a fresh sweater, Jill came out of her room. Suzi was pacing the living room, smoking a long filtered cigarette. She smashed the butt in an ashtray when Jill appeared.

"I hope you're happy."

Jill blinked. "I beg your pardon?"

"He's done it, you know, and it's all because of you."

"Done what?"

"Given up the fight." Suzi was staring at her as though Jill was completely and utterly dense.

"I hate to seem ignorant, but I honestly don't know what you're talking about."

"You're married to Jordan, aren't you?"

"Yes." They stood several feet apart from one another, like duelists preparing to choose their weapons.

"Jordan's handed control of the firm to my father and brother," Suzi explained impatiently.

"Isn't this rather sudden? When did all this happen?" Surely if Jordan was in a proxy fight, he would have said something to her. Surely he would have let her know. She'd only been away for a week. Nothing could have threatened his hold on the company in that short a time, could it?

"This proxy battle's been going on for months," Suzi snapped. "It all started while you and Jordan were on your honeymoon. He couldn't have chosen a worse time to leave. He knew it, too—that's what was so confusing. By the time he returned from Hawaii, he had a full-fledged revolt on his hands. Dad used that time against Jordan, buying shares until he controlled as large a percentage of the company as Jordan did. He wanted Jordan out as CEO and my brother in."

"What happened?"

"After months of gathering supporters, of buying and selling stock, of doing everything humanly possible to forestall a proxy fight," Suzi continued, "Jordan up and handed everything over to my father, who'll hand it all to my brother on a silver platter. You met Dean, and we both know he doesn't have the leadership or the maturity to be a CEO. Within five years, he'll wipe out everything Jordan's spent his life building."

Jill didn't know what to say. Her immediate reaction was to argue with Suzi. Jordan would never willingly have surrendered control of his company. She didn't need the younger woman to tell her that Jordan had worked his entire adult life to build the company; he'd invested everything in it—everything.

Although it seemed a long time ago, she remembered that he'd told her about buying the controlling shares. He'd also said that he'd soon be forced to battle to remain in power. Jill remembered what she'd said to him. She'd told him she couldn't imagine him losing.

"Jordan's resigned?" she repeated, breathless with disbelief.

"This morning, effective immediately."

"But why?"

"You should know," Suzi said harshly, reaching for a second cigarette and lighting it. Snapping her gold lighter shut, she blew a stream of smoke at the ceiling. "Because he's in love with you."

"What has that got to do with anything?"

"Apparently he felt it was either you or the company. He chose you."

"He sent you here to tell me?" That didn't sound like something Jordan would do. He preferred to do his own talking.

Suzi gave a short, humorless laugh. "You've got to be joking. He'd have my hide if he knew I was anywhere within a mile of you."

"Then why are you here?"

Suzi took another drag of her cigarette. "Because I fancied myself in love with him not long ago. He was pretty decent about it. He could have used me to his own advantage if he'd wanted, but he didn't. Beneath that surly exterior is a real heart. You know it, too, otherwise you'd never have married him."

"Yes..." Jill agreed softly.

"He needs you. I don't know why you left him, but I figure that's between you and Jordan. He's not the type of man to be unfaithful, so I doubt there's another woman involved. If anything, he's too damn honorable. If you don't realize what you've got, you're a fool."

Jill's emotions were playing havoc with her. Jordan had resigned! It was too much to take in. Too much to believe.

"Are you going to him?" Suzi demanded.

Jill hesitated. "I, uh..."

Suzi inhaled on her cigarette, then stabbed it out in the ashtray. "If pride's stopping you, then I don't think you have much to worry about. Eventually Jordan will come to you. It may take a while, though, if you're determined to wait him out."

"I'm going to him." Recovering somewhat, Jill looked to Suzi, struggling for the ability to speak. "I can't thank you enough for coming. I owe you so much."

"Don't thank me. I just hope to high heaven you appreciate what he's done," Suzi muttered as she picked up her purse, tucking it under her arm.

"I do," Jill assured her, leading the way to the front door. No sooner had Suzi left than Jill went looking for her mother.

She found her in the kitchen. "I heard," Elaine said before Jill could explain the purpose of the other woman's visit. "It might not last, you know."

"I'm going to him."

Her mother's eyes searched Jill's face before she nodded. "I knew that, too."

As they embraced briefly, Jill whispered, "There's a box in my room, Mom. Shelly brought it over for you—and for Andrew Howard."

The drive into downtown Seattle seemed to take forever. It was rush-hour and the only parking space she could find was a loading zone. Without a qualm, she took it, then hurried toward Jordan's office building. Luck was with her, for the building hadn't been locked yet, but she was waylaid by a security guard. Fortunately, he was the same man she'd met earlier, and he permitted her to stay.

"Has Mr. Wilcox left yet?" she asked.

"Not yet."

"Thank you," she said, sighing with relief.

She hurried to the elevator. Jordan's office was on the top floor. When the elevator doors opened, she ran down the wide corridor to the outer office where his assistants and his secretary worked. The double doors leading into Jordan's massive office were open. He was packing the things from his desk into a cardboard box.

Jill froze. She stared at Jordan for a long moment, unable to move or speak. He looked haggard, as though he hadn't slept in the week she'd been gone.

Dark stubble shadowed his face, and his hair, ordinarily neat and trim, looked rumpled.

He must have sensed her presence because he paused in his task, his eyes slowly meeting hers. His hands went still. The whole world seemed to come to a sudden halt. In that unguarded moment she read his pain and it became hers.

"You can't do it!" she cried, choking on a sob. "You just can't."

Jordan's face hardened and he seemed to clamp down on his emotions. He ignored her and continued packing away the objects from his desk. A smile, one that spoke more of sadness than of joy, came into his eyes. "Your husband is unemployed as of five o'clock this afternoon."

"Oh, Jordan, why would you do such a thing? For me? Because I left you? But you never told me... Not once did you explain, even when I pleaded with you. Didn't you trust me enough to tell me what was happening?" That was what hurt most of all, that Jordan had kept everything to himself. Not sharing his burden, carrying it alone.

"It was a mistake not to tell you," he admitted, the regret written clearly across his face. "I realized that the night you left. By nature, I tend to keep my troubles to myself."

"But I'm your wife."

He grinned at that, but again his smile was marked with sadness. "I'm new to this marriage business. Obviously I'm not much good at it. The one thing I was hoping to do was keep my business life separate from my personal life. I didn't want to bring my company problems home to you."

"But, Jordan, if I'd known, if you'd explained, I might have been able to help."

"You did, in more ways than you know."

Tears blurred Jill's eyes. She would have given everything she owned for Jordan to take her in his arms, but he stood so far away, so alone.

Jordan picked up a small photograph, one of their wedding day. He stared at it for several moments, then tucked it into the box. "I loved you almost from the moment we met. Don't ask me to explain it, because I can't. After that first night, when we kissed on the beach, I knew my life would never be the same."

"Oh, Jordan."

"Being with you was like standing in the sun. I never knew how lonely I was, how my heart ached for love, how much I longed to share my life with someone..."

Tears ran unashamedly down Jill's face.

"The day we were married," he went on, "I swear I've never seen a more beautiful bride. I couldn't believe you'd actually agreed to be my wife. I swore then and there I'd never do anything to risk what I'd found."

"But to resign..." Trembling a little, nervous and unsure, Jill moved across the room to Jordan's side. He tensed at her approach, his expression a blend of undisguised longing and hope.

"I can't lose you."

"But to walk away from your life's work?" What he'd done remained incomprehensible to Jill.

"I have a new life," he said, gently pulling her into his arms. He buried his face in her hair and inhaled deeply. "None of this means anything without you. Not anymore."

"But what are you going to do?"

"I thought we'd take a year off and travel. Would you like that?"

Jill nodded through her tears.

"And after that, I'd like to start our family."

Once again Jill nodded, her heart pounding with love and excitement.

"Then, when the time's right, I'll find something that interests me and start again, but I'll never allow work to control my life. I can't," he said quietly. "You're my life now."

"You're sure this is what you want?" He'd given up so much.

She felt him smile against her hair. "Without a doubt. I don't need a business to fill up the emptiness in my life. Not when I have you."

"Oh, Jordan," she whispered, her throat tight. "I love you so much." She squeezed her eyes closed and murmured a prayer of thanksgiving for the wonderful man she'd married.

"Shall we go home, my love?" he asked her.

Jill nodded and slipped her hand into his. "Home," she repeated softly. With her husband. The man she loved. The man she'd married.

FREE GIFT OFFER

To receive your free gift, send us the specified number of proofs-of-purchase from any specially marked Free Gift Offer Harlequin or Silhouette book with the Free Gift Certificate properly completed, plus a check or money order (do not send cash) to cover postage and handling payable to Harlequin/Silhouette Free Gift Promotion Offer. We will send you the specified gift.

FREE GIFT CERTIFICATE

ITEM	A. GOLD TONE EARRINGS	B. GOLD TONE BRACELET	C. GOLD TONE NECKLACE
# of proofs-of-purchase required	3	6	9
Postage and Handling	$1.75	$2.25	$2.75
Check one	☐	☐	☐

Name: _____

Address: _____

City: _____ State: _____ Zip Code: _____

Mail this certificate, specified number of proofs-of-purchase and a check or money order for postage and handling to: HARLEQUIN/SILHOUETTE FREE GIFT OFFER 1992, P.O. Box 9057, Buffalo, NY 14269-9057. Requests must be received by July 31, 1992.

PLUS—Every time you submit a completed certificate with the correct number of proofs-of-purchase, you are automatically entered in our MILLION DOLLAR SWEEPSTAKES! No purchase or obligation necessary to enter. See below for alternate means of entry and how to obtain complete sweepstakes rules.

MILLION DOLLAR SWEEPSTAKES
NO PURCHASE OR OBLIGATION NECESSARY TO ENTER

To enter, hand-print (mechanical reproductions are not acceptable) your name and address on a 3"×5" card and mail to Million Dollar Sweepstakes 6097, c/o either P.O. Box 9056, Buffalo, NY 14269-9056 or P.O. Box 621, Fort Erie, Ontario L2A 5X3. Limit: one entry per envelope. Entries must be sent via 1st-class mail. For eligibility, entries must be received no later than March 31, 1994. No liability is assumed for printing errors, lost, late or misdirected entries.

Sweepstakes is open to persons 18 years of age or older. All applicable laws and regulations apply. Sweepstakes offer void wherever prohibited by law. Prizewinners will be determined no later than May 1994. Chances of winning are determined by the number of entries distributed and received. For a copy of the Official Rules governing this sweepstakes offer, send a self-addressed, stamped envelope (WA residents need not affix return postage) to: Million Dollar Sweepstakes Rules, P.O. Box 4733, Blair, NE 68009.

HR2U

ONE PROOF-OF-PURCHASE
To collect your fabulous FREE GIFT you must include the necessary FREE GIFT proofs-of-purchase with a properly completed offer certificate.

(See inside back cover for offer details)

HARLEQUIN Romance®

Coming Next Month

#3199 A CINDERELLA AFFAIR Anne Beaumont
They met one stormy day in Paris—and fell in love. Their affair was brief, yet sweet and loving. It ended when Briony realized she must return to England to marry Matthew. But how can she leave Paul for a life that will have no meaning?

#3200 WILD TEMPTATION Elizabeth Duke
Bram Wild, her new boss, has a legendary reputation as a womanizer, but Mia feels sure she's immune to his wicked charms. After all, she's happy with her dependable fiancé—and why in the world would Bram be interested in her in any case . . . ?

#3201 BRAZILIAN ENCHANTMENT Catherine George
When Kate arrives in Villa Nova to teach English, the tiny Brazilian mountain town begins to work its magic on her. The same couldn't be said of her imperious employer, Luis Vasconcelos, whose rude welcome makes Kate resolve to avoid him. But that's something that proves rather difficult.

#3202 LOVE YOUR ENEMY Ellen James
They're natural enemies. Lindy MacAllister, dedicated conservationist. She's determined to protect ''her'' colony of burrowing owls. Nick Jarrett, designer of airplanes. He's equally determined to get his new factory built, on schedule and on the selected site. When the immovable object (Lindy) meets the irresistible force (Nick)—watch out!
LOVE YOUR ENEMY is the second title in Harlequin Romance's The Bridal Collection.

#3203 RUNAWAY FROM LOVE Jessica Steele
The job offer in Thailand seems heaven-sent to Delfi. She has to get away—she's afraid she's becoming attracted to her sister's fiancé! Yet, alone in Bangkok, with Boden McLaine the only person she can turn to, Delfi wonders if she's jumped from the frying pan into the fire!

#3204 NEW LEASE ON LOVE Shannon Waverly
Nick Tanner is exactly the kind of man Chelsea wants. He's dynamic, attractive and his little daughter, Katie, is adorable. Nick even seems to be sending out the right messages . . . to the wrong woman!

AVAILABLE THIS MONTH:

Take 4 bestselling love stories FREE

Plus get a FREE surprise gift!